Lizzie Dripping

Lizzie Dripping on Holiday

Helen Cresswell

illustrated by
Faith Jaques

BBC CHILDREN'S BOOKS

*For Anna, Angela and Paul
with love and thanks*

Published by BBC Children's Books
A division of BBC Enterprises Limited
Woodlands, 80 Wood Lane, London W12 0TT

First published 1974
This edition first published 1994
© Helen Cresswell 1974

ISBN 0 563 40382 9

Cover printed by Clays Ltd, St Ives plc
Printed and bound in Great Britain by Clays Ltd, St Ives plc

Contents

Lizzie Dripping
and a Birthday Wish

The Arbuckles looked at the cake. Lizzie had just pressed in the last fruit jelly to make the pattern complete. The whole cake was covered in sweets—"A rainbow cake," Lizzie thought.

"Well, I don't know," said Patty at last. "Not usual run o' birthday cakes *this* ain't."

"But I *wanted* it to be unusual!" cried Lizzie. "*Gramma's* unusual!"

"Aye. And *that* depends how you look at it," Patty said.

"It's a right pretty cake, our Lizzie," said Albert. "Good enough to eat, that looks. Try one, can I?"

He stretched out a hand and Lizzie squealed and Patty gave his hand a slap.

"Like a two-year-old!" she said. "Come to that, *cake* for a two-year-old, that looks, never mind seventy. If you'd stuck it over with mint imperials, mind. . . ."

"Well, I like it, and I reckon Gram will," said Lizzie. "Cake and sweets all rolled in one. I think them sweets stuck on is the best part."

"Come on then," said Patty, "clear it out the way. She'll be walking in that door under an hour, and nose like a bloodhound for anything she's not meant to know."

"Time for dinner, I reckon," Albert put in. "Peckish, looking at that."

"Only pity is about *candles*," said Lizzie hopefully.

"Now don't you set on about that again," Patty told her. "You get past twenty-one, you don't *have* candles. There's only you'd *think* of seventy candles, Lizzie Dripping."

Patty went to fetch a tin and Lizzie went on staring at the multi-coloured cake, but what she was seeing was a cake that *did* have seventy candles, each with a tiny pointed tip of flame, and—

"Mam!" she cried. Patty turned. "Just *seven* candles, Mam! Just something for her to blow out and make a wish."

"Aye, that'd do," agreed Albert.

Patty hesitated.

"*Please*, Mam! Might never have a birthday at our house again, Gram, mightn't."

"Not that many more, here or anywhere," Patty said.

Lizzie stared. "What d'ye mean?"

"Oh, do stop plaguing, Lizzie!" cried Patty. "And get cleared up, quick!"

Lizzie did not move. She looked at Albert, and he moved his pipe from one side of his mouth to the other.

"Getting old, your Gramma is," he explained. "That's all your mother meant."

Lizzie turned away.

"Go on, then!" she heard Patty's voice. "'Here's candles, and you'll find holders, if you have a rummage. Look sharp now!"

"Oh, thank you, Mam!"

And so Lizzie was saved from thinking what she *had* been going to think, and began instead to find candle holders, pink and blue and yellow. Even so, it was not long before she started to think again.

"Do people have to get old?" she wondered. "All of them, whether they want to or not? *I* don't want to get old. That witch, *she's* old ... bet she's hundreds of years old! Hundreds and hundreds. Wonder if ... what if I could go and see ... ? She might—I mean, *'tis* Gram's birthday. What if she'd let Gram have a wish, a real wish, that'd come true? Always ask. ..."

Lizzie nodded to herself, and put in the candles, each in a holder like a flower, making a garden that would light up later,

when the time came, more like stars than flowers.

An hour later Lizzie Dripping was waiting at the bus stop at Bilbury with such impatience that she began to feel sure the bus would never come. Her eyes positively ached with looking, so she looked away from the road and at the pit head instead, right nearby. Just then the pit siren let out its long, lonely wail, and although she had heard it a thousand times before, and although it was broad daylight and the sun shining, Lizzie gave a little shiver.

She stared at the familiar outline of the pit head, at the wheels and towers, and thought of the men down there in the dark, and though she tried hard *not* to think it, thought, "There's men down there. Miners. Right under my feet this very minute, could be." She stared down at the ground by her feet as if by staring hard enough and long enough she could actually be able to see down there.

"My Grampa died down there. Killed in a roof fall, before ever I was born. Six men, all killed. . . . Wonder what my Grampa was like? Mam says he was the salt of the earth—what's *that* mean, I wonder . . . ?"

Lizzie looked deliberately away again and stared expectantly at the bend in the road round which the bus would appear. After a minute or two she again began to have that queer, nightmarish feeling that it never *would* come.

"Like a watched kettle," she thought. "Watched kettle never boils, watched bus never comes."

So Lizzie shut her eyes. When she did not hear the approach of the bus straight away, she took further steps.

"It'll come by the time I've counted fifty," she told herself. Eyes still shut, she began counting, and had only reached eight when she heard the throb of an engine. The magic had worked.

Lizzie danced up and down as it drew up. A case and two black bags were handed down and Gramma herself at last appeared and climbed squarely and carefully down.

"Gramma!" cried Lizzie, and threw her arms about her and felt the soft, dry, papery skin, and smelt the familiar smell of eau-de-cologne and mints. (Gramma got through a bag of mint imperials every day. "Got no teeth left to rot, and good for the digestion," was what she said.)

"Hello, my little duck!" she said.

"Happy Birthday, Gram! I've got a present for you, but not till teatime, Mam says."

"Let's have a look at you." Gramma pushed her to arm's length and looked at her. "You've growed again, Lizzie, I swear you have."

Lizzie was nearly as tall as Gramma now. She often wondered that so small a body as Gramma should have produced a daughter as big as Patty.

"Near as tall as you, I am," she said.

Gramma looked round. "Where's Albert?"

"Oh, Dad's coming," Lizzie assured her. "Said we could start walking if things weren't too heavy, or else wait here. He's just gone to the shop in Bilbury for some things for the garden."

"You don't come to stop away without a bit of luggage," said Gramma.

"Oh I know. He'll not be long. Let's feel." Lizzie picked up a case and smiled. " 'S all right. I can carry this a bit. Start walking, shall we?"

Gramma nodded, straightened her hat and picked up a bulging bag in each hand. They set off, and soon had rounded the corner and were walking with the colliery tip rearing above them on their right hand like a black, conical mountain. Lizzie saw Gramma look at it out of the corner of her eye, and thought, "Poor Gramma. Must hate looking at that tip. Mam says she thinks of Grampa every time she sees it. Better say something— take her mind off it."

"Last day at school today, Gram," she told her. "I've not been at all this morning, stopped at home to help Mam with—well, to help Mam. And we've only to go back for an hour after dinner, Miss Platt says, and then we can come home early."

"That's nice," said Gramma absently. She was still thinking about Grampa, Lizzie could see that.

"And you know what—we might go to the *sea* for a day while you're here. Mam said so. Wouldn't it be smashing?"

Gramma did look interested now.

"Aye, well, that would be nice. Do with a good breath of the sea. Give me lungs a good clear out. Cough cough cough all winter I've been. Oooh—here's Albert now!"

The van drew up and Albert got out, beaming. He liked Gramma, Lizzie knew that. Next minute they were bundled into the van, luggage and all, and being driven merrily towards Little Hemlock, home, and dinner.

The school bell rang for the last time that term, and only seconds later Lizzie Dripping was out and away in the hot sun, walking home.

"All the time I want now," she thought.

And it was as if she were walking into the wide world because

11

beyond the roofs of Little Hemlock were the hills, wave upon wave of them. Lizzie knew full well that when you reached them they were just hills like any others—springy turf, daisies, scent of clover. But now they were made mysterious by distance and even looked faintly blue, though certainly they must be green.

Lizzie remembered the witch again. *She* had become more mysterious by distance. She had always been mysterious, of course, but now that Lizzie had not seen her for nearly a whole month she herself had become a little hazy, as the hills were. and beckoning. And more than a little fearful . . .

"But I *shall* see her again soon," she thought. "Oh witch—I'm coming!"

It was not just any witch Lizzie was thinking about, but *her* witch.

"I can do without the others," she thought.

She still had not forgotten that day in Little Hemlock grave-yard when all at once there had been three witches, hunched like ravens on the tomb of Hannah and Cyril Post (*Peace Perfect Peace*) all looking at her, and all a-twitch with spells.

"Just my witch," she thought. "She's different. Could've changed, mind. Never really know where you are, not with that witch."

She walked on, seeing blue hills and beckoning witches, then all at once stopped dead.

"Could've gone!" she cried out loud. "Oh no—not *gone*!"

Black and white Patch, above her on the edge of the Stokes's garden wall, started to bark and dance among the roses, and she began to run.

"I'll go and look, minute I've been home. Oooh—she must be there! I want to ask her about that wish!"

She ran then, all the way home. And as she went up the worn hollow steps to the garden there was Toby sitting in the border, and there was Gramma in a chair by the hollyhocks, dozing. She wore the felt hat she always wore "to keep sun off" and her old hands were folded peacefully in her lap and the bees made

12

paths in the air and hummed about her and Lizzie smiled a little to herself.

"Old she is, Gramma," she thought, and stood looking at her, the witch quite forgotten.

'*I'll* be old one day.' She spread her own hands and looked down at them, then back again to Gramma's which were soft and loosely veined and floury looking, almost.

"Mam first, though,' she thought. "She'll be old before I am."

Even that was hard to imagine. Lizzie shut her eyes and tried hard to see Patty with white hair dozing in a chair in the sun. It did not work. She could not even get so far as seeing Patty's hands folded in her lap, doing nothing.

"You've done, then."

Lizzie opened her eyes and was startled to see Gramma's open too, and looking at her.

"Oooh yes, Gramma. It's holidays now!"

"You'll not get far in life with your eyes shut," remarked Gramma. She picked up a sock she had been darning from a basket by her chair, and popped in a mint imperial from the bag in her pinafore pocket.

"I was only shutting 'em for a *minute*," protested Lizzie. "While I thought about something, see."

"Aye, well," said Gramma, "I do a fair deal of that myself, I s'pose, these days. Eyes shut, thinking on things, dreaming . . ."

"What d'you think *about*, Gramma?" asked Lizzie, all of a sudden curious and surprised to think that an old woman could sit dreaming. She dropped to the warm grass beside her. "What were you thinking about now—just then, when I came up?"

"Oooh—lot of old nonsense."

"Go on, Gram, tell me. You weren't asleep, were you?"

The old black-laced shoes came together as if to attention and Gramma was sitting bolt upright now.

"Go to sleep?" she cried. "Of a daytime? Me? You'll not catch *me* asleep of a daytime, my girl. Bed—that's the place for sleeping. Never been any lying about in *my* family. My old mother,

you know how old she was when she died?"

"Eighty-four?" said Lizzie, who knew.

"All of eighty-four year old. And never a nap in all her born days. 'Plenty of time for that when you're up there!'—that's what she'd say to me." And Gramma jerked her head.

"When you're—where, Gramma?" Lizzie asked, half guessing, half not even wanting to know.

"There! Up in the churchyard, under a stone. Plenty of time then for sleeping in the daytime. 'Day and night and for ever and ever till kingdom come'—that's what she used to say, and I've not forgot it. Never."

"She means it," thought Lizzie wonderingly. "You can tell she does. But she *was* asleep just now, I know she was. And I've seen her napping before, plenty of times. Funny . . . but you can't call her a fibber . . . she thinks it's true. It's only fibbing if you say a thing and you *know* it isn't true. . . ."

Lizzie heard the cuckoo far away down by the beeches.

"They call *me* a fibber, though," she thought, "and *that* isn't fair, neither. And if I was to tell them about my witch . . . !"

She sat up suddenly. The witch! Clean forgotten in that hot summer stillness held between the high hedges and the old red brick of the cottage walls.

"That you, Lizzie?" Patty's voice came through the open door.

"Yes, Mam!"

"Toby all right, is he?"

"Yes, Mam." Lizzie sighed, then got up and picked up her satchel. She went into the living-room and instead of the dim coolness she had expected, was met by air hotter than ever.

"Phew!" she gasped. "Hot in here! Hello, Mam."

She had only a cloud of steam as answer to her greeting.

"There's only me daft enough to start off ironing and baking all at one go on a day like this." Patty's hair fell damply over her face. "Birthday today, anniversary supper tomorrow. . . . Oh, I could die of it, I swear I could! Put the kettle on, Lizzie, will you, for a cup of tea. If I don't sit down soon, I shall—ooooh!"

She let out a shriek, banged down the iron and pushed past Lizzie into the scullery. There she opened the oven, snatched out a tray of tarts, faintly steaming, and dropped them onto the ironing board.

"And *now* look! Done brown and dry as biscuits and meant to be sponge! *Them* ain't going to any anniversary supper. Not having 'em say *I* don't know how to cook a bakewell. *We* shall have to eat them, for our teas, and—"

"Now what? Now what's up?"

It was Gramma, peering in at the door and sniffing.

"Nothing, Ma,' said Patty in a voice that said exactly the opposite. "You get back out and finish your nap. Just a few bakewells done a bit over, that's all."

" 'Tain't bakewells *I* smell,' said Gramma, advancing a little. Then it was her turn to shriek. "Your iron, girl!"

Patty screamed again and dived out to lift the iron. Beneath it was a towel, faintly smoking and imprinted with an iron-

15

shaped brown pattern, rather like a shield.

"Oooh! Would you *believe!*"

"If I've told you once, Patty," said Gramma righteously, "I've told you a thousand times. One job at a time." She came right in now, and started to move about in a vague way as if looking for something, all the while muttering to herself under her breath. "I dunno . . . makes you wonder if you wasn't wasting your time. All them years, year in, year out, raising kids, and—I dunno . . . times I've told you . . ."

"Out of my way, Lizzie!" cried Patty then, interrupting the flow. "And pick that satchel off the floor, will you? You'll not be satisfied till I've broke my neck over your dropped things. Bad enough going round all day after that dratted baby—and where's he? Who's minding him?"

She threw the door wide, hoping, Lizzie knew, to catch out Gramma, who had been supposed to be minding him. There squatted Toby, right out of the storm, dropping stones into his bucket to hear them clang. Lizzie stared at him dejectedly.

"Gramma nagging at Mam, Mam nagging at me," she thought. "Nag nag nag. Wish *I* was Toby. Only one round here don't get nagged at, he is. Never think it was someone's *birthday* . . ."

"Now look," said Patty, "I shall go clear out of my mind if things don't get sorted out soon. And birthdays on top of all else, and tea to lay." Here she shot another look at Gramma, who was inspecting the damage to the towel and ironing board, and still clucking under her breath. "You get Toby in his chair, Lizzie, and give him a push round. That'll be two less under my feet."

"Yes," thought Lizzie, "go and see witch then, I can, and ask her. . . ."

"All right, Mam," she said out loud.

"And fetch me some mint imperials, shall you, Lizzie, from the shop," said Gramma. "A quarter, that'll do for now. And get 'em to weigh 'em out. I don't want any of them nasty plastic bags. Here's money.' Then she lowered her voice. "And here's a few pence for yourself."

"Thanks, Gram," Lizzie took the money and gave Gramma a conspiratorial smile.

She went outside and picked up Toby, who was very dirty, and plonked him into his pushchair.

"Come on, lump," she said. "Tatas."

Lizzie often called Toby "lump" to hide how much she loved him. And she loved him mainly because he so obviously and joyously loved her.

"And you be careful!" came Patty's voice after her. "You watch out for them lorries and keep on the pavement, where you can!"

And so Lizzie set off, first walking and then at last, feeling joy coming back in a flood, running.

"Holidays, anyhow!" she thought. "And birthday tea tonight!"

She ran between the high hedges and creamy sprays of hemlock, smelling the summer and seeing ahead the narrowed blue

17

sky, all at once certain again that the holiday would be a good one. The pushchair jumped and rattled over the stones and Toby gurgled.

"Going to see a witch, Toby," she told him.

She liked Toby because she could say anything at all to him, and still get a beam for answer. And he was only two—much too young to tell tales.

"He doesn't know what a witch is, even," she thought. "Oooh, she must be there, she must! Only thing is—what if Toby's scared, or what if he yells and frightens her off?"

Lizzie slowed her pace, pondering the problem. She could not decide whether Toby would frighten the witch, or vice versa, or both. Then she felt the coins that Gramma had given her sticky in her palm, and knew at once what the answer was.

"Come on, Toby," she cried. "Got to go up to the shop, anyhow!"

Ten minutes later, hotter than ever now and out of breath, she was wheeling the pushchair into the shaded drive by the church porch.

"Here we are! Come on now, Toby, out you get!"

She lifted him up, took his hand, and Toby obediently followed her along the steep little path that led up by the church. When you started up the path all you could see ahead was the grass fringing the sky, and Lizzie thought of it as a pathway into the sky itself. Often she found herself curiously flat and disappointed to find she was at the top and still on earth, after all.

They reached the rusty iron gate that led into the churchyard itself. Lizzie stopped and listened. Her heart thudded right up in her throat.

She heard the comfortable croon of pigeons and stock-doves in the high trees, the drone of insects and a faint, never-ending whisper of leaves and grasses. She heard all the usual and familiar sounds of a summer day and yet knew in her heart of hearts that in itself that meant nothing at all. If the witch were

18

there, she would be *silently* there. She would be silently and invisibly there in the somehow greenish air of the graveyard under the yews, waiting for Lizzie alone to call her out into the world.

Lizzie drew in a deep breath and pushed open the gate.

"I must put Toby where he won't see the witch," she thought. "And her not see him, for that matter!"

Lizzie did not altogether trust the witch. She had offered once before to turn Toby into a toad, and was certainly capable of it if the fancy took her. She had turned the Briggs's cat into a toad with a mere crack of the knuckles, and had been quite tetchy about turning him back again. Lizzie looked about for a suitable tombstone as hiding place.

"That'll do," she decided, settling for *Abel Arthur Grey, Gone to Rest*, which was broad and high and not surrounded by grass and nettles as some of the others were. A stung Toby would certainly yell—witch or no witch.

"Come on, Toby, here," she said. She spoke in a whisper, though she had an uneasy feeling that if the witch were there (in whatever world of her own went on invisibly side by side with Lizzie's own) she would be able to see and hear every single thing that was going on.

"There's a good boy. Now there you are. You sit there and eat these sweeties. Lizzie'll be back soon."

Toby thrust out a grubby hand for the tube. He sat in front of Abel Arthur Grey and slowly poured a multi-coloured stream of sweets into a pile in front of him. He began to put them into his mouth, one after another. Lizzie saw that already he had forgotten her.

"That's him out the way!" she thought exultantly. "Now—the witch!"

She went cautiously down the path that led by the side of the church. When she reached the corner she stopped and peered round. Her eyes went straight to the tomb of *Hannah Post of this*

Parish and Albert Cyril beloved husband of the above 1802–1879 Peace Perfect Peace.

Nothing.

"Witch!" called Lizzie softly. "Witch! Where are you?"

Silence.

"Done this before," thought Lizzie, "pretended not to be here."

"Witch!" she called again, a little louder this time. "Witch!"

No answer. Lizzie stood and wheeled about on her shadow and raked the graveyard for a sudden snatch of tell-tale black rags. Nothing.

"P'raps she's annoyed," Lizzie thought. "P'raps she's mad at me for not coming before. Ages since I've been, it is."

"Listen, witch," she said softly, "I'm sorry I've not been lately. But there's been the school play, see, and end of term concert, and—"

She broke off. There it was! There was a rough clamour which to any casual stroller in graveyards would seem only the coarse, racketing cries of rooks. But Lizzie, who had heard the sound before, knew differently. It was laughter, the unmistakable laughter of a witch—her witch.

"Oh, witch!" she cried. "You *are* there! But where are you? I can't—"

"I spy with my little eye!" came that familiar cracked voice.

"Oooh! But I can't see you! Where are you? Please, witch?"

"Ha! Right under your nose!"

Lizzzie jumped back, and again heard the laughter, but much more faintly this time.

"Where?" she cried. "You're not going away, are you? Don't go! Come visible, witch, please!"

"Hide and seek!" crowed the witch. "Look for me, girl! Look for me!"

What began then was a mad game of hide and seek, a knee-banging unsteady running among tombstones with the grass in places nearly waist-high, and not a clue but the high cackling of the hidden witch. As Lizzie searched, part of her wanted to find the witch and part of her already wished that she had never come to the graveyard at all, that she'd let well alone while she had the chance.

"Witch! Witch!" she half-screamed at last. "I'll never find you. And it isn't fair—how can I find you if you aren't *there*?"

Her answer was a cackle from where the shade was deepest and the grass longest, and Lizzie, turning hopelessly, gasped.

"Oh! You're there!" she cried, and began to thrust her way forward knee-deep and slowly, as if wading through water. As she went she kept her eyes fixed on the witch, and so she actully *saw* her disappear. First a high, malicious cackle, then a dissolving of that thin face and those twitching black rags into— nothing! She dwindled like smoke into the sunless gloom that was always under those particular yews on even the hottest summer day.

"Oooh!" Lizzie was furious now. "You cheat, you cheat!"

She stamped uselessly (for what use was a stamp that could not be seen for undergrowth?).

No answer.

"Gone!" thought Lizzie. "Sure as eggs—gone."

She stood for a moment longer and then began, very slowly, the long climb up the graveyard. She made for the path, away from the nettles. She walked with her head bent, angry at having been cheated, but even sadder because it seemed now as if she had lost her witch for ever.

"And all my own fault, I suppose," she thought.

She lifted her head then and drew in a sharp breath, because there, right in front of her, was the witch, thoroughly at home now, sitting where she had so often sat before on the tomb of the Perfectly Peaceful Posts. She went on knitting quite unconcernedly as if the game of hide and seek had never happened at all.

Lizzie took a little step forward.

"It's nice to see you again, witch," she offered—not altogether sure that she meant it, at that particular moment. The witch was even trickier than Lizzie had remembered—not so safe, more

likely to spring sudden spells. This was a toad-turning mood she was in, if ever there was one.

"Hmm!" sniffed the witch. "Easy enough to *say*!"

"But it is nice!" cried Lizzie. "I mean it!"

"Hmmm! Then where've you been? Eh? Answer that! Forgotten me, hadn't you? *I* know!"

"No, I hadn't, really I hadn't!" cried poor Lizzie. "I've been meaning to come the minute school broke up. And the holiday only started an hour ago, and here I am already! So I *must've* wanted to see you, mustn't I?"

"Not manners." The witch was talking to herself now. "Here one minute, gone the next! Not manners."

"*She's* a fine one to talk!" thought Lizzie incredulously.

Aloud, she said: "But I'll come every day and see you now, honest I will. Every day."

"Easy to say," returned the witch, unmollified. Then, lifting her head and looking so hard at Lizzie that she actually began to back away: "Every single day? Rain or shine? Good or ill? Hell or high water? Come what may?"

Lizzie swallowed and nodded.

"Promise?" The witch shot her head forward startlingly, and Lizzie found herself up against a tombstone.

"P-promise."

The witch sank back like a raven into its feathers.

"Hmm. Good." A finger stabbed out and Lizzie jumped. "Not saying I'll be here, mind! *I* ain't made any promises."

Dumbly Lizzie shook her head.

"Might be here—might not. Depends. But mind you are."

Lizzie nodded. She swallowed.

"Ask her," she thought, "now. . . ."

"Witch," she said carefully, "it's my Gramma's birthday today."

The witch took no notice.

"She's seventy. I've decorated her cake, with sweets and that, and candles. . . ."

Still the witch ignored her.

"And I've made her a present as well. Knitted her a tea-cosy, a yellow one, with a blue bobble."

"Hmm!" cried the witch. "Don't believe in birthdays."

"Don't you?" cried Lizzie, delighted. "Don't you really? I bet you're hundreds of years old, and I bet *you* don't get older—not *really* older, I mean. . . ."

The witch shrugged.

"Don't get birthdays," she said. "*I* don't get no tea-cosies."

"So don't you think," Lizzie was very careful now, "don't you think it'd be nice if *Gramma* didn't have any more birthdays? I mean, didn't get *older*—stopped how she is, like you do."

Again the witch shrugged.

"Up to her," she said.

"Oh but it isn't," cried Lizzie. "It's up to you! She can't *help* getting older, see, not like you can. But what if . . . what if you was to do a spell, or if you was to give her a wish. Then she could *wish* for that! Oooh, could you? It'd be like a birthday present for her. . . ."

The witch, uncommunicative as ever, knitted and mumbled.

"You'd like my Gramma, if you met her," said Lizzie. "Honest, you would."

"Grammas," replied the witch briefly, "is folks' own businesses."

"Have you got a gramma?" Lizzie was gape-mouthed at the very thought ("*Thousands* of years old, *she'd* be!" she thought).

"If I had a gramma, she'd be my business, and if I hadn't she wouldn't," said the witch obscurely.

Lizzie tried again.

"But you *would* like my Gramma. Bit like you, she is, in a way." She had a sudden inspiration. "And . . . and she *loves* knitting—always knitting, Gram is!"

"Well I don't!" snapped the witch, and Lizzie saw that she had said the wrong thing. "Spelling's what I like. Can she?"

"Can she what? Oh, no!" said Lizzie craftily. "She isn't *half* as clever as you. That's why I thought you might give her a wish, see."

The witch preened, and Lizzie pressed her advantage.

"And—and I could knit *you* a tea-cosy as well, if you liked. You give her a birthday wish, and I'll give you—"

She broke off. The witch seemed to have stiffened, and was looking beyond Lizzie at something over her shoulder.

"What's that!" she snapped, and almost in the same instant Lizzie heard a familiar voice and froze with shock.

"Hello!"

It was Toby, saying "Hello" to the witch. (He said Hello to everyone. He'd say Hello to Jack the Ripper himself, so Patty always said.)

"Oh!" cried Lizzie, her mind a-spin with pictures of toads. "Toby!"

She turned towards him and then back again to the witch to implore her not to change Toby into a toad, and—

Gone!

"Hello," said Toby again. There was mud *and* chocolate all

25

over him now. He looked like some kind of mucky little cherub with his tight silver curls and blackened face. He beamed at Lizzie and she ran to him, light-headed with relief.

"Oh Toby!"She took his hand: "Just look at you!"

They began to walk together out of the graveyard. But there was one thing Lizzie had to be sure of. She stopped and knelt in front of Toby so that their eyes were on a level.

"Toby—did you see that witch?"

He looked back at her with his clear blue eyes and said nothing at all, and she was certain, absolutely certain, that he had no idea what she was talking about. He had seen—perhaps—an old lady dressed in black knitting in the graveyard. And there was nothing unusual about that.

Lizzie picked him up and whirled him round, and cried: "Come on, Toby, quick! Birthday party now, and cake! Yippee!"

They did light the candles, later, just before Gramma cut the

cake. (Not that she did not think *that* a pity. "Too good to cut, this is," she said, "by half!")

"All right," agreed Lizzie. "But you must blow as well. Hard. And wish, remember! Wish! Now—one, two, three!"

They blew, and the candles went out, every one of them, leaving a definite little darkness for a moment, like that after a firework has gone out.

"I wished," said Gramma softly, nodding to herself. "I wished. . . ."

And Lizzie was satisfied. Because after all, witch or no witch, *everyone* is entitled to a birthday wish, if they can blow out the candles.

Lizzie Dripping
and the Little Angel

Lizzie was sitting on a rug in the garden stuffing a green silk frog with rice when Aunt Blodwen came up the path. Towser got up and barked at her. He had never got used to Aunt Blodwen, or else did not want to.

"Morning, Lizzie," she said. "Keeping an eye on your brother, are you?"

Toby was digging, as usual. All you could see of him was his bottom, his heels and his white floppy sun-hat.

"I'm making this frog," said Lizzie. "Toby's all right."

"Keeping an *eye*, though, I should hope," said Aunt Blodwen. "And trying to be a help to your Mam. Supposed to save work, great girls like you, Lizzie, not make it."

Lizzie did not answer. There was never much point in holding a conversation with Aunt Blodwen. It was like being up against a high stone Welsh wall. She contented herself with thinking "Sorry for *her* kids, if she had any," and held up the finished frog. He flopped beautifully, and she could feel the rice slithering under the thin green silk that was his skin.

"Two buttons for your eyes, and you're done, frog," she told him. "Take this lot in, better, before Toby gets among it."

She gathered up the odds and ends of material, stuffed them into the scrap bag and went indoors. Patty and Blodwen were already sitting with cups of tea.

"*Smell* a cup of tea going, can Aunt Blod," thought Lizzie.

She put the bag on a chair and went to the mantelshelf for the button box.

"Not there, Lizzie!" cried Patty. "Up to your room, if you please! I don't know—holiday hardly started and cluttering up house already. Now do start as you mean to go on, our Lizzie, else you and me'll be falling out, I can see that."

"All right, Mam." Lizzie took the button box, picked up the scrap bag and made for the stairs.

"All the same, kids," she heard Patty say. "Though I daresay you and me was no different, Blod, in our time."

"Oh, I don't know." Blodwen's high Welsh voice floated up the stairs, as doubtless it was meant to. "Quite a help to my Mam I was, as I remember. Proper little housewife. But one of seven I was, see. Makes a difference, you know."

"Oh yes," thought Lizzie. "We all know about *that*. What's she doing round here anyway? Something's up, *I* know. . . ."

She tossed the scrap bag on her bed, took the box of buttons and went and sat on the top stair. There she started rummaging for a pair of matching frog's eye buttons, and listened to what was going on down below.

". . . lovely little lad he is," she heard Aunt Blodwen say. "Proper little angel. And not a scrap of trouble, Megan says."

"I daresay you'll enjoy having him, Blod," came Patty's voice. "Be a bit of company for you, having none of your own."

"Through choice, Patty, through *choice*," Blodwen reminded her. "Told Arthur, I did, right from the start. And no *children*, Arthur, I said. Like things neat and tidy I do, and as they should be. Not all that mess and clutter children make, and the noise into the bargain. Neat and tidy and nice and quiet, that's how I like it."

"Oh, I know, Blod," agreed Patty. "You've always said. And I'm bound to say I can't see you with kids—no offence, of course."

"And none taken, Patty," came Blodwen's voice, tight and high.

30

"But you'll enjoy having this little lad a week or so—what did you say his name was?"

"Jonathan. Lovely name, Jonathan. Got a bit of class to it, that name has. And ten years old—her eldest, see. Lovely child, she says, and not a scrap of trouble from morning till night."

"*I bet,*" thought Lizzie. "What's she on about? These'll do. Look good, that frog will, with yellow eyes." She shut the button box and went down.

"Our Lizzie'll help you out with him," Patty said. "Won't you, duck?"

"Won't I what?" asked Lizzie, knowing perfectly well.

"Your Auntie Blodwen's got a little nephew coming. Your Uncle Arthur's just gone to fetch him. Ten years old. John his name is."

"Jonathan, Patty," said Blodwen. "Jonathan."

"Well—near enough," said Patty cheerfully. "You can't be coming out with a mouthful like Jonathan every time you speak. Anyhow, you could help out a bit, Lizzie. Get him to know the other kids, and that."

"Aye, well . . . we shall have to see," said Aunt Blodwen. "Thank you for the tea, Patty." She got up, clutching her handbag to her. She always carried it like this, as if she were all the time afraid of being robbed.

"Thinks I'll get him into trouble," thought Lizzie. "That's what she thinks."

"We shall have to see," said Aunt Blodwen again. "Got her hands full with her own brother, I daresay."

"Oooh!" shrieked Patty. "I clean forgot! What's he up to!"

She flung open the door and there was Toby, still squatting in the border, putting stones in his tin bucket to hear them clang.

"Ah, bless him!" cried Patty fondly. "He's hardly moved this past hour. Going to be like his father, Blod, you can see that. Can't get Albert out of the garden, you know. He'd live in that greenhouse, if you'd let him."

"Gets hisself *dirty*, though, don't he, Patty?" said Aunt Blodwen dubiously. "Just look at him!"

31

"Ah, bless him!" cried Patty. "Bit of dirt don't hurt, do it, my lamb? Give your Aunt Blodwen a kiss then, shall you, my pet?"

Blodwen clutched her handbag more fiercely than ever (using it as a shield now, Lizzie thought) and edged quickly past Toby and on down the path.

" 'Bye, then!" she cried. "See you soon, Patty!" and her sensible heels clacked away over the stones.

Lizzie grinned.

"That did it," she thought with satisfaction. "Good old Toby."

"I don't know. . . ." Patty was staring after Blodwen, wiping her hands on her apron, not because they needed it, but because it was a habit she had.

"Don't know what, Mam?"

"Your Aunt Blodwen. How she'll get on with that little lad. No more idea about kids than flying kites. . . . Still, not our worry, I suppose."

32

"Do her good," suggested Lizzie. "She don't know how the other half lives. You said that yourself, Mam."

"Why, you little . . . !" Patty laughed despite herself. "What's that you're making?"

"Frog." Lizzie held him up by his hind legs.

"Ugh!" cried Patty.

"Just going to put his eyes on," Lizzie told her. "Yellow eyes, he's going to have."

"Well, as long as you don't let Toby get hold of them." Patty was already turning back into the house. "Feel as if I've swallowed a few buttons myself, this morning."

"Don't you feel well, Mam?"

"Oh, I shall live, I daresay. Keep an eye on Toby, shall you, while I get on? Your father'll be back to dinner and I'm all behind as it is."

And so the morning passed, and Lizzie made another rice-filled frog, so pleased was she with the first. This time he was of yellow crimplene with red eyes, but he was not so froggy as the first because the rice did not slither under her fingers through the crimplene as it did through the silk.

At dinner time over the steak-and-kidney pie and peas Patty told Albert about the little angel. "Oooh, she's in for something like a surprise," she said. "I've yet to see the lad that's an angel—nor the lass either, for that matter."

"Present company excepted, of course," said Albert, and winked at Lizzie over a knifeful of peas.

"Oooh!" Patty rolled up her eyes and threw up her hands, and even Lizzie, in all honesty, was bound to say: "Not an *angel*, Dad, not me. Don't think I should like that much, anyhow."

"I should bet my last tenpence," said Patty, getting up and stacking the plates, "that he'll be round here to be from under Blod's feet before he's hardly had time to unpack his things."

"What's he coming for, then?" enquired Albert. "Give his mother a rest?"

"Well—you know," said Patty meaningfully. She lowered her

33

voice. "More a *family* matter, Albert. Mum going into hospital. *You* know."

Albert looked puzzled for a moment, then his face cleared. "Oh. Aye, I see."

"And so do I," thought Lizzie. "His Mum's having a baby. Why don't she say so? They never still think I think babies get found under gooseberry bushes. Toby didn't, that *is* certain."

Toby was gravely pushing peas about in the gravy swimming in the tray of his high chair.

"Gramma got her bus all right, did she?" asked Albert.

"Aye. She'll not be back until five. Likes a good rummage round shops, does Ma, though what she finds to need at her age, I don't know."

"Er—what d'ye say I take Toby with me this afternoon?" he suggested. "Give you a break."

"Oooh, I wouldn't say no," said Patty, as if Toby had been under *her* feet all morning, not Lizzie's. "Be all right, will he?"

"Putting in a new bath at the Cobbses," said Albert. "And you know her. Daft as a brush about babies, is Elsie. Give you a chance to get off and do something as well, Lizzie. What'll you do this afternoon?"

"Oooh . . ." Lizzie pulled her helping of tart towards her. "I dunno, Dad. But I'll think of something. . . ."

By the time Albert and Toby went off an hour later, Lizzie had thought of something. The house and garden were very quiet now. Patty had gone to lie down. This was something she very rarely did, and Lizzie was glad that Gramma was off in Kipton and not to know about it.

"We should only get all that stuff about sleeping on in the day, and graveyards," she thought, and immediately regretted thinking it, because the word "graveyard" to Lizzie meant only one thing.

"Did promise that old witch," she thought. "And kept it, I have, all week. And she wasn't even *there*, yesterday."

Lizzie, for once, did not want to go to the graveyard. What she wanted was to go to the lake at the bottom of Larkins' garden and lie there in the rowing boat under the trees, reading.

"After all—could perhaps nip down to the graveyard after tea," she told herself, though she knew that this was not at all likely. She went to the bottom of the stairs and called up softly: "Mam! Mam!"

There was no reply. The only sound in the house was the heavy ticking of the clock, and even that seemed a drowsy, hot-summer-afternoon ticking, as if time were deliberately going more slowly than usual, the miser clock hoarding the golden hours against the winter. Lizzie looked at it, and listened. Then quite deliberately she took off her wristwatch and laid it on the table.

"Don't *want* to know what time it is," she thought. "Not this afternoon. Now what? Best leave a note, I s'pose."

She was glad that her mother was asleep. Every now and then Patty had qualms about letting Lizzie go in the boat, though she had promised never to untie it when she was there alone. She simply stepped into it, in its mooring place under the trees and lay there, reading, dreaming, dipping her hands in the cold water—savouring it with her fingers.

Lizzie wrote *Gone to Larkins* on a scrap of paper and left it on the table under the teapot. Then she took her book and a cushion and went quietly out. Towser got up and stretched and wagged his tail. Lizzie patted him.

"Can't, old chap," she told him. "You'd only jump in, or something, and chase them ducks."

At the end of Church Lane Lizzie looked out of the corner of her eye towards the graveyard, but again thought "Don't matter—always go later"—and turned left instead of right. She was still half looking the other way and so banged right into the boy. She stepped back, thought "Who's that?" and then he said:

"You Lizzie Dripping?"

Lizzie instantly collected herself. "Penelope Arbuckle, my name is," she told him.

"That's right—Lizzie Dripping. My Auntie Blod told me. Said you'd got pigtails and a turn-up nose, and you have."

"Oh—you're Jonathan," she said.

He nodded. He did look rather like an angel, Lizzie was bound to admit, with his fair hair and round face. It was not his fault, of course, that Blodwen was his aunt. This was a misfortune that might have happened to anyone, and Lizzie sympathised with it.

"I was coming to your house," he said. "She told me to. I wanted to climb the trees, but she wouldn't let me."

"No," Lizzie thought, "she wouldn't." She was sorry for him. But more than anything she wanted to be away on her own in that watery world under the willows, and so she said: "Sorry, I can't play now. Got to go somewhere, see. But I will later, honest."

"After tea?" he asked.

"Got to have my hair washed. Tomorrow. I'll see you tomorrow. *I* know some trees we could climb."

He looked at her, then at the book and the cushion. Lizzie

hoped that she was not turning red, because it was a kind of a fib she had just told him.

"Sorry," she said again.

He shrugged. "It's all right. I'll find something."

So Lizzie, feeling mean and small, went on down between the steep banks of Mark Lane and when she reached the bend, turned and looked back. The boy still stood there, looking after her, though he immediately turned away.

The Larkins were not at home. Mrs Larkin always went to market on Fridays and her husband was at work. Slowly Lizzie walked under the trees by the water's edge. It was cool under there, a special, delicious summer cool, all the better for the knowledge that in a single step she could be out of it again and under the hot sun. She sniffed the cold, inexplicable smells of the water and weeds and ferns and was happy to be alone there with the whole afternoon ahead of her and time something only to be forgotten.

The thought of the witch, perhaps at this very moment waiting invisibly in the graveyard for Lizzie's visit, floated to the top of her mind again and she pushed it down.

"Doesn't matter," she told herself yet again. "Go tonight, I will." And if Patty would not let her (Friday really was the night she always washed Lizzie's hair), then it would not be her fault.

"Ooooh!" Lizzie stopped dead and a little gasp flew from her lips.

For a moment, for a single moment, she had seen the witch— not the witch herself, but her reflection in the thick green water-mirror below. Lizzie whirled to look back over her shoulder.

"Couldn't have been," she told herself. "Can't have a reflection if there's nothing there to *be* reflected."

Shaking her head to emphasise the truth of this, she came to where the boat was moored and stooped to pass under the low boughs. She came to the lake's edge and there, staring up at her, was the witch in the water again!

"Oh!" Lizzie straightened and caught her hair in a branch and ducked again and lost a pigtail by its roots, or so it felt.

Lizzie crouched there, right near the damp grasses and with flies and insects drawn to her warmth like moths to candles. Was her witch a new kind of being now—a witch-in-the-water? And if so, was she still there, actually live and solid (if ever a witch can be said to be either of these things)? Was she *there*, in the sense that a mermaid is there in the sea? Or had she now become a mere reflection—because a reflection, thought Lizzie, is only really another name for a shadow. A shadow on water. The difference is that a land-shadow is only a silhouette, but a water shadow is a painting, a real portrait, with depth and colour and real stares from real eyes.

"I'll try," thought Lizzie. "See if she *is* still there—can talk."

"Witch!" she called softly. "Witch, are you there?"

There was no reply, and nor, though Lizzie stared ever so hard and long, was there the merest deep-down glimmer of a witch's shape in the quiet green water. All at once there was a flapping and squawking and Lizzie leapt to see the Larkins' ducks and moorhens thrown into a flurry on the other side of the lake.

"Not a fox," thought Lizzie, "not this time of day. A—witch?"

The birds shrugged their wings down again and gathered themselves back into their proper shapes and the place went very quiet again. Lizzie regarded the boat.

"Shall I, or not?"

An afternoon afloat in that quiet spot had become quite a different prospect with the possibility now of a witch in the willows.

"Witch!" she said loudly and abruptly, crossly even, because her pleasure was being spoilt. "Witch, if you're there, come on out!"

But the witch did not come out. And because it is difficult to feel both afraid and angry at the same time, Lizzie shrugged her shoulders, tossed her book and cushion into the boat and herself climbed carefully down after them.

Immediately the feel of the afternoon came flooding back to her and things were just as she had imagined them and wanted

them to be. She smiled and arranged her cushion and lay propped there for a while and without even opening her book. She trailed a hand in the icy water. She stared up through the swarming green and gold yet dusky air to the sky beyond the boughs, and even the whistle of birds was green and liquid. Her happiness was so real that Lizzie felt she could have wrapped it up, if she had wanted, and put it in her pocket, to keep. She felt the gentle sway of the boat and could hear all the water sounds about her, the sucks and plops and splashes that gave away the life that was happening even in that quiet pool. She stared and listened and in the end drifted, quite naturally, into a kind of dream. . . .

Lizzie woke with a start. She opened her eyes, then shut them straight away against the dazzle. She struggled upright and the boat swayed dangerously, and once she was sitting up with her eyes open again she saw at once that she was adrift. Stupidly she stared about her. The bank was far away on all sides and the sun beat down and she thought fleetingly "Like the Ancient Mariner!" Then she thought, "The witch! It *was* her, after all!"

Fearfully she scanned the undergrowth, seeing in her mind's eye how that witch must have come creeping down, stooped above Lizzie's own sleeping form and then slowly, wickedly, untied the knotted rope. . . .

"Best get ashore, anyhow," she thought. "Quick, before she sees me!"

She bent for the oars. They were not there.

"Gone!" Her hand flew to her mouth. She was properly adrift now on that tideless pool, could stay there motionless and spellbound for ever if she were not rescued.

"What'll I do? What if Mam has—? What time . . . ?" Her eyes went to the blank white mark on her wrist where her watch had been. "Oh . . . oh . . . !"

She tried to paddle then, with her hands, furiously. But all that happened was that the boat went round and round in little rocking circles and she felt the cold water flying up and soaking through her shirt.

"Can't get out," she thought, "can't *swim*. . . . Weeds, Mrs Larkin says—ooh, and a great fish with snapping teeth—a pike! Old Nick, that's what she calls it—and they've all seen it, all the Larkins. Says it's been there in the mud on the bottom for years, growing and growing, and eats all her little ducks it does, every spring. Like a kind of monster . . . have your arm off, she says. Jaws like a nutcracker. . . . Oh!"

She scanned the quiet surface of the pool for the hint of a wicked black fish and wondered fleetingly if it were not a witch fish, in league. . . . She wrapped her arms about herself and sat helpless while the boat gently swung itself into motionlessness again.

"What if Mam doesn't see my note? What if the Larkins don't get back till late? What if—what if they've gone off on their *holidays*? Could've. . . . Ooooh, and what if that fish comes up of an evening to feed, like the cows do?"

40

She pictured the dusk falling, the gnats hanging in low clouds over the water, the slow fade of bird-song, the evil fish coming up from his muddy bed, lurking, circling, grim jaws a-twitch.

"Ooooh!" she quavered. "I'm frit, I am!"

The golden dream was gone into nightmare now.

Then for the second time that day fear changed in a single moment to anger.

"That witch!" she thought fiercely. "Spiteful thing she is!" Then, "Witch!" she half screamed. "You come on out! D'you hear me? You come and get me off this lake this minute!"

There was no reply. The sky hung motionless in the lake. Lizzie stared. There—again—mirrored in water but invisible in air, that infuriating witch.

"Witch!" She really was screaming now. "Witch!"

The reflection sank to the bottom of the pool—or whatever reflections do when they disappear.

Lizzie was half sobbing now. She brushed a hand angrily across her eyes and looked about for help—inspiration—anything. And she saw, incredibly, a moving blue shape beyond a bush on the nearest bank.

"Hey!" she cried. "Help! Help!"

The bushes parted and a face peered through. It was the boy.

"Ooooh—I—it's you! Thank *goodness*! Help me, won't you? I'm stuck out here and no oars and Mam'll be missing me soon and—"

"How did you get out there then?" he asked. "Without oars?"

"Ooooh—*I* don't know! *Do* something, won't you. Please?"

Still he made no move.

"You were yelling just now," he said. "I heard you. You were yelling 'Witch!' What witch? I don't see any witch. And who believes in witches anyway? Don't tell me—"

"Shut up!" hissed Lizzie over the water. "Be *quiet*, won't you?"

She took a quick scan over the lake, fearful that reflections had ears.

"All right,' said the boy, "keep your hair on."

41

"*Do* help,' she begged. "That rope, there by the tree. It's ever so long if you untie it. You untie it, and throw it out."

He nodded and started towards the tree.

"Funny," thought Lizzie fleetingly, "not told him which tree yet, and he knows. What if . . . ? No. Why should he? Any case, I saw that witch . . . her all right!"

"Here you are—catch!" shouted Jonathan, and threw the rope. It fell a long way short.

"Tie a knot in the end," Lizzie instructed him. "A big knot. That'll make it go further."

He struggled with the wet rope and Lizzie watched and felt ashamed already of her suspicions. He threw the rope again. It fell only just short. And again. Then again. That time Lizzie caught it.

Elated, she cried, "You've done it! Oh *thanks*!"

"Pull now, shall I?"

"Let me just sit properly—wait. That's it. Now, pull."

He pulled. The boat swung smoothly into the bank. A little thud and she was as good as home and dry.

"Tie it round again, shall I?" he asked, and she nodded. She picked up her book and cushion and tossed them ashore. As she prepared to climb out herself Jonathan came and held out a hand.

"I can manage," said Lizzie. "It's all right. I'm used to it."

But he still held out his hand and she took it, or thought she did. Afterwards, she could not remember what happened except that the boat lurched under her, she threw out an arm to regain balance and next minute went into the water, headlong.

"Oooh!" she shrieked, and spray flew in a blinding mist and in it she thought she glimpsed the witch. And the water was icy and she screamed again because of the cold and the shock and the swift picture she had now of a snapping black pike with teeth like saws—Old Nick.

How she got out was a mystery, too. Jonathan seemed to be helping and yet not helping, shouting and leaping and pulling, then letting go and grabbing again. It seemed to take a very long while. Even wet to the bone as she was and spluttering, and even jumbled among visions of the state of her sandals and of Patty's face, came the thought "He's enjoying it!"

On the bank she shook herself like a wet dog. It had little effect. She felt like a waterfall.

"Home," she thought dully.

Clutching her book and cushion she began the long squelch home. Jonathan came too, but spoke only once.

"You'll catch it," he said, half-way up Mark Lane, and left her at the corner.

Numbed now by disaster, it did not surprise Lizzie to meet Gramma by the stone steps, arms full of parcels, hat awry.

"Lizzie!" she screamed. "Where you *been*?"

"F-f-fell in the lake," chattered Lizzie. "And oh Gram, Mam'll kill me!"

"You'll have the pneumonia!" shrieked Gramma. "That's what you'll have! Quick, girl!" and she gave Lizzie a push up

the steps with her black pastic shopping bag. "And what's *she* doing?"

"In b-b-bed," said Lizzie, "p-p-poorly."

"In bed!" cried Gramma. She pushed past Lizzie now and marched on ahead. "Nice thing. If that don't beat all. Lying in bed and her child half drownded! Whatever's got into her?"

She threw open the door, then turned. "You get them shoes and socks off," she ordered, "and wait."

Lizzie bent and did as she was told.

"Now get in and stand on here," ordered Gramma, reappearing. She laid a towel on the floor. Thankfully Lizzie stepped inside.

"And now off with the lot!" said Gramma. "And rub yourself with this!" She tossed in another towel and went to the foot of the stairs.

44

"Patty!" she called. "Patty!"

There was no reply.

"Asleep!" Gramma was disgusted. "My own flesh and blood and the way *I* brought her up. *I* don't know. I really don't know. You stop there and I'll fetch things out your drawer. No need to tell her. Only make the devil's own fuss, and a fine one to talk, I must say."

"B-b-but my hair," quavered Lizzie. "It's s-soaked."

"We'll wash it,' said Gramma tersely, and began to climb the stairs with her square, flat-footed tread.

Lizzie, towelling herself in a daze, began to feel warmth and relief running together through her veins.

"Of course!" she thought. "Friday night—hair washing!"

Her glance fell on her watch, lying where she had left it.

"Almost as if I'd *known* I should fall in. . . ." she thought. "Queer . . ."

Mechanically she picked it up and held it to her ear. It was ticking sweetly.

"Dead, you'd've been, watch, if you'd've been on my wrist this afternoon," she told it. Then she pulled the towel round her and Gramma appeared with a jumper and jeans and Lizzie smiled at her and Gramma, shaking her head, actually smiled back. . . .

Lizzie Dripping

Tries a Spell

Lizzie Dripping was busy tempting fate, as usual. It did not *look* as if she were. It looked as if she were simply shredding petals from a daisy and playing the old game of "He loves me, he loves me not." But the game Lizzie was playing was far more dangerous. She was playing "witch or not".

Yesterday she had not been to the graveyard at all. Instead she had broken her promise, and fallen into Larkins' pond. Today she was not sure whether she could face the witch, and was plucking a daisy to decide for her.

"Witch—not—witch—not—witch—*not*!"

Delighted that fate had come down exactly in line with her own inclinations, Lizzie jumped up.

"That's it, then—not!"

It had not, after all, been her decision, but the daisy's. She went round into the little orchard and sat in the swing. Up she went, and the world began to seesaw, went all sloping and different. She hung back her head and gazed at the undersides of leaves and boughs and thought what mysterious things apples were, and wondered what it would be like to be a bird.

"Smashing," she thought. "Swooping about all day and sleeping in trees. Bet it's lovely in a tree at night, all rustly, like rain on your window. Wonder what it feels like, flying . . . bit like swinging, I s'pose."

She heard a hoarse caw, like that of a crow, and thought, "Not a crow, I shouldn't be, if I was a bird. Something pretty, something all—a swallow. Yes, that's what I'd be. A swallow."

The swing all of a sudden seemed to be soaring and swooping like a swallow, very fast and high, and again Lizzie heard that rough cry and knew in the instant that it was not a crow at all.

"The witch!" she gasped and turned her head to look and thought she glimpsed a snatch of black in the greenery and tried to slow the swing so that she could jump off.

"Turn *me* into a crow, she would, for two pins," she thought, and was even relieved to hear Aunt Blodwen's voice.

"Patty! Are you there? Patty?"

Lizzie had slowed right down now so that she had her feet on the ground again, and sat waiting.

"She'll have brought that boy," she thought. "*Said* I'd play with him today, so s'pose I'd better."

"Lizzie!" It was her mother's voice now. "Lizzie!"

"Coming!"

She went slowly through the grass and noticed three cabbage whites clinging to the warm bricks, basking. When she rounded the corner she saw Aunt Blodwen, the boy and Patty standing there looking at her.

"And what's all this I hear?" cried Patty. "All this about falling in ponds? And why wasn't I told, you sly little madam, and what about those new shoes? Where's your shoes?"

Lizzie looked at Jonathan and he looked innocently back.

"You sneak," she thought. "You *sneak*."

"I've got them on, Mam," she said, advancing a little, as if to prove that they still worked. "They're all right, honest. And I was only on the *edge*, Mam, when I fell in. Couldn't have drowned."

"Right in the middle!" cried Aunt Blodwen. "Right in the middle she was, and without oars! And to think our Jonathan might have been out there with her and heaven knows what happened. And what'd I've said to Megan, I ask you, with her little child left in my keeping, and drownded!"

"But he's not drowned," said Lizzie. Like most people whose

imaginations carry them away she was irritated when other people's did the same. Also, she wished Jonathan *were* drowned.

"You shush up!" cried Patty. "Never mind who's drownded and who ain't. Not the *point*! Times I've told you about going on that pond! You'll not go again, my lass, that's certain. And after what you'd promised, Lizzie, that's worst of it."

"I didn't row out, Mam," said Lizzie desperately. "Honest. I sat in the boat, and fell asleep, and when I woke there I was—right in the middle. *I* don't know what happened!"

All three stared at her.

"It's true, Mam!" she cried.

"Oh, very likely," cried Aunt Blodwen, "you'll be telling us next that—"

"Now what? Now what?"

It was Gramma, blinking in the strong sunlight, a little dazed and bad-tempered-looking, as if she had just woken up. Not of course that she could have—not in broad daylight.

Patty rounded on her.

"And *you* must have known!" she cried. "And that'll be why you washed her hair—and me thinking it was out of kindness, with me being poorly."

"Such a fuss!" snapped Gramma. "Lizzie fell into the pond and I dried her. What's to do about that?"

"And why wasn't *I* told? I am her mother, aren't I?"

"You? Snoring in bed, you was, and in broad daylight. Who'd've dried her if I hadn't've been there, I should like to know? The pneumonia, that'd've been the next thing. You can still die of it, you know. *Oh* yes, for all their clever penicillins and medicines. Woman up *our* road got took with the pneumonia last year, and *she* died of it!"

Gramma, triumphant, stood hands on hips, and Patty wilted a little and Lizzie saw that the tables had been well and truly turned. She even began to feel sorry for Patty now.

"Never mind, Mam," she said encouragingly. "I ain't got the pneumonia, I'm *sure* I ain't. I feel fine."

"Then you don't deserve to!" snapped Patty ungratefully.

"Oh well," said Aunt Blodwen, "no use crying over spilt milk, I s'pose."

"Yes," thought Lizzie, "and who *spilt* it!"

"Leave Jonathan here a bit then, shall I, while I get on?" she went on brightly. "Flowers to do, see, for chapel. My week, this week."

"Up to you, Blodwen." Patty gave a bitter laugh. "Don't go leaving him here if you think he'll end up drownded."

"Oh!" Blodwen forced a gay laugh. "Won't do that, will he? And Lizzie'll have learned her lesson now, I daresay. Wouldn't've mentioned it to you otherwise, see. Only reason was I thought it was my duty. 'If you don't tell Patty, Blodwen,' I says to myself, 'and that poor child gets herself drownded, you'll never forgive yourself.' So I tell you, see."

"Hmmm." Patty seemed no more convinced of Aunt Blodwen's good intentions than Lizzie herself was. "Well—it's

49

up to you, I s'pose. I shall have to get on. Work to be done, even if you are fit to drop."

She turned and went in, shooting a sideways look at Gramma as she went. There was an uncomfortable pause.

"Oh well—that's fine, then, isn't it?" said Aunt Blodwen, still being bright. "You stop here, Jonathan, and play with Lizzie for a bit. Dinner at one sharp, mind, and don't get yourself dirty."

She went a few paces down the path, then turned.

"And no *trees*, Jonathan," she said. "No broken necks, not in my house, thank you."

All three watched her go down the path, off to go round people's gardens snipping flowers with her sharp Welsh scissors.

"*There* goes one that'll never fall in a pond," remarked Gramma.

Lizzie looked sideways at Jonathan's expressionless face.

"He never thinks I'm playing with *him*," she thought. "Not *now*."

"That woman," she heard Gramma's voice, "always puts me in mind of a toothbrush."

"A—who? Aunt Blodwen?"

"A scrubby little toothbrush," nodded Gramma. "Busy-bodying about."

"Oh Gramma, you are daft!" Lizzie giggled. "Makes you want to bare your teeth, you mean—like this?"

Lizzie bared them with relish.

"Don't know what I mean," said Gramma enigmatically. "Just does, that's all. No more than that. No whys or where-fores."

With that she lost interest and turned to follow Patty indoors. She paused. Her hand went to her pinafore pocket.

"Mint imperial?"

Lizzie nodded and took one, and Gramma went in.

"She never gave me one!" said Jonathan, astonished.

"I don't expect," Lizzie told him, "she wanted to."

"But you always offer round!" He was thoroughly astounded

as if a law of nature had been reversed—fish started flying or owls hooting at noon.

"Why?" asked Lizzie.

Jonathan was temporarily floored.

"Well—you just do," he said lamely at last. "It's manners."

"Oh, *them*," said Lizzie. "Well, I only give sweets to them I like, and I expect Gramma's the same. I don't think she noticed you, as a matter of fact."

She turned on her heel and went back to the green comfort of the orchard, in the hope of salvaging what was left of the morning. She sat on the swing and immediately saw Jonathan peer from behind the corner of the cottage. Pretending not to notice, she lay back as far as she could, looking upwards again, scanning the boughs for unborn apples.

"Drat him!" she thought, finding that she could not think

while she was being watched. "Why doesn't he go away?"

He did not go away.

"Wish *I* could spell," she thought. "*I'd* spell him!"

Suddenly she stretched out her whole body, seized by an idea, an idea so terrifying and awesome and yet so glorious that she could not imagine why she had not thought of it before. She flew like an arrow now, stiff with excitement.

"What if she could *teach* me! I reckon *I* could be a sort of a witch! P'raps I am, already. After all, nobody sees her, except me. Don't think so, anyhow. I bet that's it! I bet it's because I'm a bit of a witch myself. I know, I'll test it out. I'll shut my eyes, and spell that witch to be . . . to be in Farmer Stokes's hayfield. Then I'll go and look, and if she *is* there, I'll *know* I'm a witch! And then I'll ask her—ask her about spelling!"

"Can I have a go?"

Lizzie sat up. He was right by her now. She stood up.

"You can have a go," she said with extreme sweetness. "You can have a go all morning. It's all yours."

"Where're you going?" He caught up with her. "Can I come?"

"Nowhere," said Lizzie.

"What're you going to do, then?"

"Nothing."

"You said we could climb trees."

"That," she told him, "was before somebody went telling tales."

"She asked me where I'd been, so I told her."

"Yes. *And* you knew she'd come straight round telling. Spying old busybody!"

"You shut up about my Aunt Blodwen!"

"Oooh—Auntie Blodwen's little boy, are you now? You go away and play like a good boy, and mind you keep yourself clean. No climbing trees, mind!"

"And your Gramma's a rude old woman, saying she's like a toothbrush and then not handing round sweets!"

Lizzie laughed then with pure delight.

"Hee—a toothbrush! She is rude, my Gram. We're all rude at

our house. You keep away and you'll be all right."

She started to go in earnest now, leaving him behind.

"What *are* you going to do?" he shouted after her.

"I told you!" she called over her shoulder. "Nothing!"

"That's all there is to do round here!" he shouted after her. "Nothing! Horrible place this is. Boring rotten little place! Glad I don't live here!"

Lizzie turned for the last time.

"And so am I," she told him. "So *that's* lucky, ain't it? Come on, Towser!"

Now she really did go off, down the garden path and into Church Lane, and as she went she heard his voice after her:

"Lizzie Dripping, Lizzie Dripping,

Don't look now, your fibs are slipping!"

"Didn't take him long to learn *that*!" she thought furiously and began to run, not because she wanted to get out of earshot of the chanting (she had heard that a thousand times before)

53

but because she felt certain that he would try to follow her, as he had done yesterday.

She slipped inside the open gate of the hayfield and flopped breathless behind the hedge. Towser did the same. There, Lizzie lay doing nothing at first but draw in the smell in gulps, the smell of new-mown hay, freshly turned and giving off its heady scents under the hot sun. It smelt like a fresh grass tastes when you chew it. Lizzie picked a lush stalk of grass from the shadow of the hedge and bit into it and the sudden sweetness burned her tongue. She sat up, all at once alert.

"What's that?"

She crouched behind the hedge and looked through. Jonathan was coming, stamping his feet as he came and chanting in time: "Auntie Blodwen's a scrubby old toothbrush, Auntie Blodwen's a scrubby old toothbrush . . ."

Lizzie clapped a hand to her mouth to smother her laughter. He was level with her now, only a few feet away through the hedge.

"Auntie Blodwen's a scrubby old toothbrush

And Lizzie Dripping's *worse!*"

He stamped his foot hardest of all on the last syllable and Lizzie's mirth gave way at once to fury.

"Lizzie Dripping's *worse!*

Lizzie Dripping's *worse!*"

"Where's he going?" Lizzie wondered. "Looking for a tree to climb, I'll bet! He'll catch it! Hope he does, and all!"

She sat back on her heels then and remembered why she was there.

"Don't seem to be here, that witch," she thought. "Could be hiding, of course. Say something out loud, I'd better. Say it something like a sort of spell. Let's think . . ."

She sat cross-legged then and drew herself up very straight backed and shut her eyes tight.

"Witch appear, witch appear!

I make you witch, out of the air!"

It came so easily that she surprised herself. So much like a

real spell did it seem that when she opened her eyes she was certain the witch would be there. Not a blink or snatch of black in
sight. She let out a long sigh of disappointment. Her eye fell on
a daisy.

"See what the daisy says. Sort of spell, that is."

She held the daisy in her left hand and began to nip off its
petals one by one with her right.

"Witch—not—witch—not—witch—not—witch—!"

Lizzie sprang to her feet. As she did so the skylark's song
went out like a candle flame and instead she heard a familiar
cracked voice:

"Toad—not—toad—not—"

It was the witch, enthroned on hay, plucking a daisy with
those long white fingers. Lizzie blinked. It was like seeing the
witch for the first time, seeing her black cloak spread on spiking
hay, her whole impossible person in so wide and sunlit a place.

"It worked!" she thought incredulously. "She's here!"

"Toad—not—toad—not—toad—*not*!"

The last fierce syllable shot Lizzie to attention.

"Pity," said the witch, and tossed the bald daisy into the air.

"Oh witch!" cried Lizzie then. "I spelled you here, and here you are!"

The witch smiled, not a real smile, at Lizzie, but her usual one, to herself.

"Hgh!" she cried. "And where were you yesterday? Eh? Eh?"

Lizzie stared back at her.

"But you know!" she thought. "You were there! It was you as—"

"I was *there*!" cried the witch, as if reading Lizzie's thought. "I know, I saw. . . ."

"But I was coming to see you later," cried Lizzie, "and I would've, really I would, if you hadn't've—"

She broke off. She did not dare accuse a witch.

"What?" The witch leaned a little nearer. "What?" she prompted. The word was a hoarse whisper.

"You—" Lizzie gulped—"you know—undid the rope, and—and made me fall in!"

The witch gathered herself then. She drew in her robes, she stretched and straightened.

"I—did—what?"

Lizzie flinched from the last spat syllable.

"Y—you were there! I saw you!"

The witch looked at her then, long and hard.

"Wherever you see me, there I am," she said musingly, half to herself. "Which is witch, you or me?"

"There you are!" cried Lizzie. "*You've* noticed, as well! That's what I wanted to see you about. You see, I think—well, I know it sounds daft, but I think *I* might be a little bit of a witch, myself . . ."

"You. . . ." murmured the witch.

"And what I *really* wondered," went on Lizzie, "was whether you could teach me to do a bit of spelling."

The witch said nothing.

"It came to me, all of a sudden," she went on. "Best idea I've

ever had in my whole life. Think, to spell!"

"Hmmm. Think it easy, do ye?" cried the witch.

"Oh no!" cried Lizzie hastily. "Oh no, witch, I don't think that! It's just that—ooh, if you could spell, you could do anything you wanted in the whole world! Like fly, for instance—fly like a bird—turn yourself *into* a bird, for that matter."

"I'm bird, times," crooned the witch. "I'm bird I'm cat I'm toad I'm shadow-in-the-water. A rare slippery one I am."

"Oh you are!" agreed Lizzie. "And I know I could never be as good at spells as you are. But if you could tell me just one, just *one* for me to try. . . ."

The witch gazed at her for what seemed a very long while and Lizzie crossed her fingers and hoped that she was not thinking dangerously.

"*I* know what it is you want," the witch announced at last. "You come a little closer, and I'll whisper."

"You will?" Lizzie could hardly believe it. "Oh *thank* you, witch!"

And she went forward and was suddenly right close up against the witch, within inches of that supernatural flesh, that elusive huddle of black rags. The whisper came. Lizzie nodded. The witch whispered again and Lizzie stepped back, dazed.

"Oh!" she exclaimed softly. "I've a spell to do! I'll do it—right away I will!"

"Wait!" snapped the witch. "Not so fast, my girl. There's reckonings to be made yet. You made a promise."

Lizzie nodded.

"Them that break promises," said the witch softly, "pay forfeits."

Lizzie's eyes widened.

"Forfeit?" she repeated at last in a small voice.

"Break a promise, pay a forfeit," nodded the witch, almost happy now. "And me to choose. *I* choose the forfeit!"

"Oh dear, oh dear!" Lizzie felt herself once again to be on the very brink of toadhood.

"Let's see," murmured the witch, "what shall it be . . . ?"

"Quick! Think of something yourself, Lizzie, before she does!" then, out loud,

"Climb the chestnut by the Adamses—*that's* hard! Break your neck doing that, Mam says."

The witch nodded slowly.

"Climb the chestnut and bring me back a green spray from the seventh bough. A green spray, for working spells."

"Long way up, *that* is," said Lizzie, "seventh bough."

"Or shall I think of something else?"

The witch, black and solitary in that wide golden landscape, was an inescapable fact, forcing Lizzie to decision.

"I—I will, then," she gulped. "I'll fetch it."

The witch, satisfied, sank back and rocked herself on the gently creaking hay. She surveyed Lizzie, considered her.

"Tricksy, you are," she murmured. "And you break promises. You bring that bough to me. Bring it tonight. You hear?"

"I—hear. In the graveyard?"

58

"Dusk. Owl-light. Come at dusk. And mark this!"

A crooked white finger stabbed and Lizzie waited. "Them that break two promises," said the witch softly, "pay two forfeits. And there'd have to be spells. I should have to do some spelling, if two promises were broken."

"Oh, I'll come!" cried Lizzie. "I will, honest! But don't—"

The witch went melting into hay. Witch—black mist—hay. Gone. The skylark throbbed and spun a long way up and all Lizzie had for comfort was the heat, the sun burning companionably into her skin. She shivered a little as she went through the gate and into the lane and walked like a sleepwalker down towards the Adamses. After a time she felt better, and remembered the spell. She said it inside her head, savouring it, and smiled.

"To think! A witch!" The thought was irresistible. "To fly at night like an owl! Go invisible on people's heels, to stop clocks ticking! Yes—*that's* the first thing I'd do—stop clocks! It'd be summer then, all year round, and Gramma'd never grow old, not ever. And flowers—them buttercups there, for instance— they'd stop open, for ever and ever. Oooh—the things I'll do if I do turn out to be a witch!"

"Lizzie!"

She came to all at once.

"Lizzie? Thought you was playing with Jonathan. Where's Jonathan?"

I don't know, Aunt Blodwen," said Lizzie innocently. "Said he wanted to climb trees—wanted me to show him some. But I wouldn't."

"Trees!" cried Aunt Blodwen. "I should think not, indeed! Better not let me catch him climbing trees!"

"Not used to it, he isn't," said Lizzie. "Break his neck, I should think—bound to."

"Oh!" shrieked Aunt Blodwen.

"His leg, anyhow," went on Lizzie. "If he didn't break his neck he'd break his leg. Or arm. Or something. Bound to."

"And tear his trousers into the bargain, I shouldn't wonder!"

cried Aunt Blodwen. "After all that was said to him. Won't I tan his backside!"

"Didn't say he *had* gone climbing, Aunt Blodwen," said Lizzie. "Just thought he might've. Don't suppose he would, really—I mean, little angel like he's meant to be. And you told him not to."

"You go and look for him, Lizzie," said Aunt Blodwen. "You go this minute!"

"Oh I can't!" said Lizzie. "I'm on a—I'm on an errand. Doing an errand for an old lady."

The witch was, after all, old, if not entirely a lady.

"Oh. Oh. Well, then, you keep a *look* out for him, Lizzie Dripping," said Aunt Blodwen. "And if you see him, just you tell him that his Aunt Blodwen wants him this minute. *I'll* give him climbing trees."

"I'll tell him," promised Lizzie, and off she went again.

"Another thing I could do if I was a witch," she thought. "Get Aunt Blodwen spelled into something and out the way. Spider, she'd make. Yes, that's it, a spider. Spider in the bath, and wash her down the plughole!"

She laughed aloud at the thought and ran the rest of the way to the Adamses. Her gaze went straight to the great chestnut whose seventh bough she was to pluck as forfeit.

"Do the forfeit first, better," she thought, "and then the spell. Just you wait, mister sneaky Jonathan, *I'll* spell you, in a bit!"

She advanced towards the tree.

"Lizzie! Lizzie!"

The voice was coming from the tree. "Well!" thought Lizzie. "He *is* up a tree! I *am* a witch, I'm *sure* I am!"

"You'd better come on down out of there!" she called up. "Your Aunt Blodwen's looking for you. Going to tan the backside of you, she says."

"I can't!" came the voice, muffled by leaves. "I'm stuck!"

"He's *stuck*!" Now Lizzie really could not believe it. "I haven't even *said* the spell yet, only practised it, inside my head. And he's stuck! Oooh—I *am* a witch!"

"Can you get a ladder?" came the voice.

It suddenly struck Lizzie as comical, this talking tree, and what with that and the staggering proof of her own witchhood, she laughed out loud.

"Can't!" she said. "Adamses are out. Don't you like it up there? Where are you?"

She went closer and looked right up through the layering boughs and could see Jonathan's face, white and boggle-eyed, in among the leaves like some rare bird.

"Not scared, are you?" she asked.

"No! No, course not. I just want to get down, that's all."

"I'll tell you what," said Lizzie thoughtfully. "I'll run and fetch your Aunt Blodwen. *She'll* think of something."

"No! Oh no—don't! Please!"

Lizzie sat down then, where Jonathan could see her.

"P'raps—p'raps you could come up and help," came the

voice. "You're good at climbing trees."

"Oh, I am," agreed Lizzie.

"Got to go up, anyhow," she thought, "to fetch that forfeit."

Her eyes fell on a daisy, and she stretched out for it.

"Tell you what," she said, "I'll ask this daisy. See what it says."

"Ask a *daisy*?"

For answer Lizzie began to nip off the petals one by one.

"Tree—not—tree—not—tree—"

"Are you barmy, or something?"

Lizzie paid no attention.

"Tree—not—tree!"

She shrugged and got to her feet.

"I'm coming," she said.

Lizzie had climbed the chestnut tree before, though never higher than the third fork, where she had found she could actually lie along the bough, her back resting against the trunk, and fancy herself a bird, or just dream. When she reached this point, she looked up.

"Four, five, six, seven," she counted. "Nearly at the *top* that looks!"

Jonathan himself seemed to be on the next bough up, the fourth. Next minute she was on a level with him. A few inches higher, and she would be able to reach the seventh bough. She heaved herself up.

"Hey!" cried Jonathan. "Where are you going?"

"Got it!" Triumphantly she let herself down again, a spray from the magical seventh bough clutched in her hand.

"Phew!" She had no pocket, so she put the twig between her teeth.

"What on earth?"

"Now—down!"

She hung on with her hands and lowered the rest of her body carefully. Her toes sought a foothold and failed. Her feet hung in space.

"Help!"

She felt a hand clutching at the back of her shirt, and next

moment was up on a level with Jonathan again.

"See," he said. "You can't get down. Get up all right, but not down."

"Move over, can you," said Lizzie. Then there they were, both sitting side by side, "Like a pair of love birds," she thought, and giggled.

"Not funny," Jonathan said. "Hours we could be stuck up here."

"One thing," said Lizzie. "I'll not get into trouble. Only came up to help you."

"So what did you go on further up for then?" he demanded. "And what's that twig for?"

Lizzie eyed him.

"Do you believe in witches?"

"Witches?" His voice was incredulous.

"Well, do you?"

"Course not."

Lizzie looked sideways at him, hunched on his bough, thoroughly miserable and headed for certain doom, and was almost sorry for him.

"Your Aunt Blodwen'll murder you." She spoke her thoughts out loud.

"If we ever get down," he said gloomily.

"Could be up here all night if no one comes!" Now it was Lizzie's turn to be alarmed. She began to wish that she had kept her spells to herself. This particular spell seemed to have rebounded in a very unwitchlike way.

"My bottom hurts," Jonathan said. "Ages I've been up here."

"Not torn your *trousers*, I hope?" enquired Lizzie.

For answer Jonathan stretched out a leg bare almost to the knee, the trouser falling away from the seam.

"Crikey!" she exclaimed. "You did!"

There was silence then.

"Serves me right, I s'pose," Lizzie thought. "Got what I asked for, all right. Kept on about being a bird, and now I'm stuck up a *tree* like a blessed bird. Nothing to write home about, either."

"I wonder how long it *will* be," came Jonathan's voice. "Before someone finds us, I mean. I s'pose your dog wouldn't go and fetch someone?"

Lizzie shook her head. She could see Towser, head on paws away down below, oblivious and content.

"Might go home when he's *hungry*," she said. Then, "Let's play something. That's what miners do, trapped in a pit. To keep spirits up, see, and pass time. Let's play a guessing game, or something."

"I spy?" suggested Jonathan.

Lizzie heard a voice inside her head, the witch's voice. "I spy with my little eye!"

"Shall we?"

"Oh—oh! Yes. All right," she agreed.

"I spy with my little eye," began Jonathan, "something beginning with . . . g . . ."

An hour later they were still playing, and were beginning to run out of ideas. There was not very much to see from where they sat.

"I spy with my little eye, something beginning with . . . h. . ." said Jonathan.

"Hungry," said Lizzie instantly. "And I am. Ravenous. Dinner time, near. Mam'll go mad. And sausages, it was."

"Bet Aunt Blodwen won't give me anything," said Jonathan glumly. "Not even if we do get down, I mean."

"Never mind," Lizzie told him encouragingly. "I could bring you a few bits, out pantry. Come to our house, you could, and then Gram'd mend your trousers for you."

"I wish I'd never pushed you in pond," Jonathan said.

"You—what?" Lizzie turned on the bough to face him. "*You*?" Jonathan stared back.

"But you knew!" he cried. "You must've! Who else could it've been?"

"But I thought it was the w—" Lizzie's voice died away. "It was a rotten mean thing to do," she said.

"I know. I'm sorry, really I am."

"Listen!" hissed Lizzie, clutching at his arm.

Footsteps. Whistling.

"Help!" they both shrieked together. "Help!"

The footsteps and the whistling stopped.

"Up here!" cried Lizzie. "Up in the tree!"

"Well, if it ain't our Lizzie!" came a voice, and Lizzie really did shriek then.

"Dad! Dad! Quick. We're stuck up tree!"

Next minute Albert's face was staring up at them through the boughs.

"Eh, well," he said. "Stuck, are you?"

We've been up here hours, Dad," cried Lizzie. "Get us down, can't you? It's near dinner time!"

Albert was nodding.

"Came to do guttering for Mrs Adams," he said. "Got ladder in back," and disappeared.

"Oooh!" breathed Lizzie. "Thank heaven!"

"And leave spells alone, I'd better," she thought. "Bounced back on *me*, that one did."

Then Albert was there again, and she cried, "I spy with my little eye, something beginning with—l! And bags first down it!"

And she was, down the ladder and coming out of the tree, not in a flutter of wings like the bird she had longed to be, but one foot after another like the Lizzie Dripping she really was.

Lizzie Dripping
and the Treasure Hunt

"Have we *got* to take Toby, Mam?" asked Lizzie, pulling on her wellingtons. "You can only go on the roads, with pushchair. I want a proper walk."

"Here," said Gramma, waving her umbrella at Lizzie's boots, "*I've* no boots, and shouldn't put 'em on, if I had. Not traipsing across fields, not at my age, thank you."

"Not in *fields*, Gram," said Lizzie. "On the footpaths. You'll be all right. I know *lots* of paths."

"Hark at 'er!" cried Gramma. "*Born* here, my lass, seventy odd years back. More footpaths than there was roads, then. I could show you a few paths, if I was minded."

"Can we leave Toby then, Mam?" asked Lizzie again, and Patty nodded.

"Go on then, pair of you. I don't know which is daftest. And mind that dog don't get filthy wet, like he did yesterday. Comes in here, wags his tail and that's wallpaper all splattered up. Then he wipes himself across my tights, and he's dry and it's *me* that's wet. You keep an eye on him, Lizzie."

"Oh, I will, Mam," promised Lizzie. "He's ever so good, really."

"Oh aye," said Patty. "I've seen him. Comes bounding up that garden like a blessed stag. Oh well! If he comes home wet he can always stop out till he's dry."

So Lizzie and Gramma set off.

"Not too far," said Gramma as they turned into Church

Lane. "She's right—rain about. Black as Harry's knitting bag over yonder," and she jerked her head in the direction of the church.

Seeing the church must have set off a new train of thought, because she said next: "Lot of folk I know, in there," meaning the graveyard.

"Someone *I* know, and all," thought Lizzie, meaning the witch.

Gramma crossed Kirk Street and plodded steadily into the churchyard.

"Oh, Gram," cried Lizzie, "you're not going in there now!"

Gramma paid no attention. Instead of taking the little grass path into the sky she marched towards the other gate that led into the graveyard, not more than a few yards from the tomb of the Perfectly Peaceful Posts.

"Oooh!" Lizzie's head went into turmoil. "Witch'll think it's me come to see her, and what if she's there, what if—?"

With relief she saw that the witch was not there—not visibly, at any rate, and in her usual place.

"Hgh!" Gramma stopped and looked about. "Now—where've they put Polly?"

"Polly? Polly Summers, you mean, *Only Sleeping?*" And she saw, horrified, that the witch was there, right behind Gramma. Lizzie shook her head and pulled a face, and the witch grinned and stayed exactly where she was.

"That's her," nodded Gramma, "where is she?"

"She's down there, at the bottom end, but it's all nettles and long grass and that. Come on, Gram, let's go for a walk like we said!"

"What's her stone like?" demanded Gramma.

The witch was beckoning now, and Lizzie shook her head again and frowned warningly.

"Lizzie!" snapped Gramma.

"S-sorry, Gram. Oh—her stone—you know, just ordinary. But big—big it is."

"Ah!" cried Gramma triumphantly. "I knew it! It would be.

68

That woman, she'd always to have biggest and best of anything there was going. Always to go one better, that was Polly Summers, and same dead as she was alive, by the look on it."

She paused and stared down the long path through the graveyard and her whole face changed.

"You stop here, Lizzie," she said. "I'm just going down yonder a minute."

Off she went, a sturdy black figure seeming to wade in the long buff tide of grass, and Lizzie thought, "Gone to see Grampa...."

Then she remembered the witch and turned to see if she were still there. She was. "I didn't *come* to see you," Lizzie told her. "It was *Gramma* came. Go away, won't you, and I'll come back later."

"Stop if I want," said the witch huffily.

"But she'll see you!" cried Lizzie.

The witch smiled wickedly and did not answer.

"Oooh—sometimes I get fair *sick* of you!" cried Lizzie then.

"Hoity toity!" reproved the witch. She wagged a finger. "Hoity toity! You that *brought* me here, remember, in the first place!"

"You don't seem to *realise*!" went on Lizzie. "It's all right for you—all you've to do is flit about all day, spelling, and that! *Live* in the graveyard, you could. But it's different for me. Got a life to lead, you know, and—oh!"

The witch had gone. She had melted suddenly into the green without warning, gone as though against her will, banished by a spell of her own making.

"Oh—now I've gone and upset her," thought Lizzie. "Gone into one of her huffs. But it's true—I can't be at her beck and call the whole time."

It did not even occur to her that perhaps it was the witch who was at her back and call.

"You be careful!" Lizzie jumped at the voice out of thin air. "You—be—careful! I could *go—for ever!*"

"Come on, then." It was Gramma, and she kept walking.

69

"Not all day to moon about in graveyards."

Thankfully, Lizzie followed, and once back in Kirk Street again she breathed a sigh of relief. She liked walking about Little Hemlock with Gramma, but it was usually more like a triumphal procession than a walk, punctuated by long chats, by stepping inside cottages for cups of tea, and waves left and right. Gramma had lived all her life in Little Hemlock up to six years ago when she had left to live near one of Patty's sisters who kept a little shop and needed help. Gramma knew everyone—even the handful of new-comers, whose histories she pieced together from second-hand snippets of information, so that by the time she actually did meet them they too seemed like old friends, and she would greet them as such, to their bafflement. Everyone Gramma met, she spoke to.

Today, Lizzie wanted Gramma to herself, which was why she had suggested walking along footpaths.

"Let's go up to the Braille wood, Gram," she said now. "Up through the allotments, over cow pastures and that."

Gramma nodded and went briskly on. Up the little jitty they went, and past the post office to the allotments, without meeting a single soul. Working on his allotment, was Jack Jackson. He did not see Lizzie and Gramma, and they stood there, staring.

"Where's it gone?" whispered Lizzie at last. "Footpath—it's gone!"

Gramma drew herself up.

"Jack!" she called. "Jack Jackson!"

He straightened up then, and turned.

"I'll have a word, if you please," said Gramma.

Jack Jackson, whom Gramma had known from childhood ("thievingest, slyest little brat in the village," she said) came now to her bidding. He advanced, at least, a few paces.

"Morning, Mrs Bailey," he said. "Grand day."

Gramma did not agree with him, and he coughed and grew uncomfortable in the silence.

"Not matter even if we have a drop of rain," he offered. "All

70

right for lettuces. They'll not want umbrellas." He gave his humourless laugh.

"Lettuces," said Gramma grimly, "is neither here nor there. Where's that footpath?"

"Aye. Well . . . you see, Mrs Bailey," he began.

"I do not see, Jack Jackson," interrupted Gramma. "There's a footpath—" she gestured with her umbrella—"*there*, that's been there since I was a little child. That's been there, Jack Jackson, for hundreds of years. Hundreds and hundreds and hundreds."

Jack Jackson, evidently dazzled by this unreeling of the centuries, merely scratched his head and looked at his lettuces.

"And *now*," went on Gramma, "it's gone to lettuces!"

"Aye. Well . . . you see, Mrs Bailey," began Jack Jackson again, "there's no real *call* for footpaths, you see, not these days. You got to *cultivate* land, see. Up the yield. Hundreds lettuces up, I am, without that path cutting straight through."

"Listen you here," said Gramma. "It's no difference if you're a thousand lettuces up. It's no difference if you're a *million*. You get that path put back. And quick!"

Jack Jackson looked helplessly at her and then back at his careful rows of vegetables and Lizzie could see that he was wondering how you put a path back, quickly. Then he seemed to rally, and straightened up and said with something like a show of spirit,

"No *harm* done, Mrs Bailey. No other complaints, there's been. If you was wanting to get to the cow pastures, you could always go the back way, see, up Tenter's Lane. Else you could come up here, see," he indicated the path that ran up the side of his garden, "and then get to the stile along back, if you was careful not to tread on my lettuces."

"I'll give you tread on your lettuces!" cried Gramma. "*I* ain't going tramping through soil, not at my time of life. And I know my rights, what's more. *Law* against digging up footpaths, and the law's what I'll have on you, Jack Jackson, if you don't get that path put back quick!"

"Aye, well," said Jack Jackson, "that's putting things a bit

strong. There's other paths gone from round here, besides this, you know. You got to move with the times. Progress."

"Don't you stand there telling me about progress!" shrieked Gramma. She waved her umbrella then. "Don't you go turning six pennorth of lettuces into progress, not in my hearing. And I'm warning you, Jack Jackson. If that footpath ain't put back where it belongs by tomorrow morning, there'll be steps taken."

Jack Jackson, speechless, stared. Even Lizzie could not help wondering whether Gramma thought the path had been rolled up, like a stair carpet, and could be put down again as easily.

"Come along, Lizzie!" snapped Gramma, and off they went, back the way they had come, the walk over.

"Drat Jack Jackson and his blessed lettuces," thought Lizzie. "That's our walk spoilt, thanks to him."

At dinner time Gramma held an inquest on the missing footpath.

"Don't know what you're making such a fuss about," said

Patty. "Not the end of the world."

"Aye, Patty," said Albert, "that's whole point. Folks don't make fusses, and footpaths go. There's dozens gone from round here, that *I* know about. *You* might not like walking, lass, but there's plenty do."

"My teacher says that," put in Lizzie eagerly. "Miss Platt—she says we've all to look after the countryside. Nation's heritage, that's what she calls it."

"All *I* know is," said Patty, "that if folks like that Jack Jackson can make a bit extra by way of digging up footpaths, dig 'em up they will. That Jack Jackson'd dig up his own *grandmother* for lettuces."

"Against law, though, Patty," said Albert.

"Aye, well, that wouldn't bother him overmuch, either," returned Patty sourly.

"Means there's something we can *do* about it, though, Patty," said Albert, quiet, but kindled too.

"Oooh, what, Dad?" cried Lizzie.

"Stamp on 'em," said Gramma briefly. "Stamp on his blessed lettuces. *I* will!"

"Not *stamp*, Gramma, not exact," Albert told her. "Something more—planned, like. What they did at Mapleburn last year. What you do, see, is organise a proper walk, a walk on the footpaths, for everybody, like."

"Oooh—I remember!" Lizzie cried. "And they made it into a treasure hunt, with a picnic. Mary Bell went from our school, and she said it was smashing. Won second prize she did—a paperweight it was, all out of glass!"

"That's the kind of thing, Lizzie," nodded Albert.

"And who's to organise it, pray?" demanded Patty. "As if I needed to ask."

"Wouldn't be that big a bother, Patt," said Albert apologetically. "Bit of an interest, in fact. Put clues in rhymes we could, like they did at Mapleburn."

"Rhymes!" Patty laughed. "You?"

"Like—like for instance . . ." Albert cleared his throat:

73

"Take the turning to the right
And a stile will come into your sight."

They stared at him, every one of them, and it was Patty who broke the silence.

"You made that *up*?" she asked. "This *minute*?"

"Well. . . ." Albert cleared his throat again. "Aye."

"Well!" Patty was astonished. "I should never've known you'd got it in you. What was it again?"

"Take the turning to the right
And a stile will come into your sight."

Albert repeated it diffidently, trying to hide his pleasure in his unexpected success as poet.

"Well! If you can do it, Albert, you do it," cried Patty warmly then. "I never!"

"We could all help," put in Lizzie. "*I* can think of a rhyme as well:

Run until your feet do tingle

74

And find a clue inside the Pingle!"

"Lovely!" cried Patty, clasping her hands.

And, "Aye, that'd do," agreed Albert. So the whole thing was settled. A footpath walk, which was to be a Village Treasure Hunt and Picnic would be organised for one Saturday afternoon. Only the Arbuckles themselves and Miss Platt, the schoolmistress, were to know the clues, and where the treasure lay.

"Oooh yes, Miss Platt'd help, all right," Lizzie told them. "Only thing is, with me being in on it, shan't be able to win prize, shall I? What'll prize be, Dad?"

"Oh—summat," he replied. "Ask Miss Platt, you could—see what she thinks."

And so began a rhyming time for the Arbuckles. Rhymes went to their heads, they seemed to be rhyming even in their sleep. Even Patty was caught up in it. Lizzie found her one morning up to her elbows in suds, staring out the window and saying:

"When you come to Cherry Tree
On the gate a clue you'll see!"

over and over again, as if unable to believe in her own powers.

Miss Platt provided ten of the clues and promised to help lay the trail the night before. She also said that she would give the first prize. Gramma did not altogether approve of Miss Platt because she was against stamping on Jack Jackson's lettuces.

"What we must do," Miss Platt said, when Lizzie told her about the missing footpath, "is walk between them by all means, but as carefully as we can. Remember, Lizzie 'The purpose of war is peace'. You can disagree with a neighbour without there being any spite about it."

Gramma, when Lizzie repeated this precept to her later, was unimpressed. Lizzie felt sure that Gramma, who after all was no pupil of Miss Platt's, would stamp on Jack Jackson's lettuces willy-nilly. In fact, so far as Gramma was concerned, this was the sole purpose of the exercise.

Lizzie and Jonathan, now firm allies for the time being,

made posters to put in the Post Office and on the notice board by the Memorial Hall. There was to be no charge for entering, and it soon became apparent that on the day fixed for the Treasure Hunt, almost the entire population of Little Hemlock would be tiptoeing through Jack Jackson's lettuces. Not, of course, that they knew this. As far as they were concerned, this was to be a Treasure Hunt and Picnic, and they all wanted to be there.

The night before the Treasure Hunt, Lizzie, who had spent the evening helping Miss Platt to lay the trail, was sure she would never be able to go to sleep. Patty came up as usual to turn off her light and tuck her in, and Lizzie asked her: "Are you excited, Mam?"

"Excited? Whatever about?"

"You know—treasure hunt, and that."

"Oh—that!" Patty pulled the blankets tight. "Take more'n that to excite me. And what you've to be excited about I don't know. You know all the clues, don't you?"

"Mmm. Helped Miss Platt put 'em down. Wrote 'em all in indelible ink she has, case of rain."

"And that wouldn't surprise me," said Patty. "Now get off to sleep."

She kissed Lizzie, turned off the light, and went downstairs. Lizzie lay there, wide-eyed in the half dark.

"Won't rain," she murmured. "Lovely, it'll be . . . ooh, and picnic in the buttercup field. . . ."

She lay seeing pictures of bright acres, blinding gold with buttercups. She pictured herself roly-polying down the steep grass slopes of Hell Hills, and before long her pictures dissolved into dreams. She was asleep.

Lizzie was woken by the bell of her alarm clock, set for eight o'clock. She put out a hand automatically to turn it off, then lay there, luxuriously coming to.

"Oh—today," she thought, "it's today!"

Still she lay, and became aware then of a light rustling, a steady pattering, a—wide-awake in an instant, she scrambled down her bed and pulled aside the curtain.

"Oh no!"

The rain went rolling down the window in great pear-shaped drops and the view of the church and the green was blurred and misty. Lizzie stared for a few seconds then ran downstairs. The others were already up and drinking tea.

"Oh Mam, Dad—look at it! It'll ruin it!"

"Well, I did say," said Patty, as if her prediction of rain had in some mysterious way produced it.

"You take no notice," said Gramma. "Needed a drop of rain, didn't we, Albert?"

"But the Treasure Hunt!"

"Rain before seven, fine before eleven," said Gramma, unperturbed.

"Oh—you never believe that!" Patty was scornful.

"If you'd lived as long as *I* have, my lass," said Gramma, "*you'd* believe it."

Patty, who had *not* lived as long as Gramma, said no more.

"Could only be a shower, Lizzie," said Albert. "Early yet. *Do* with a spot o' rain, like Gramma says. Ground's fair cracking with dryness. And hunt don't even start till two. Can't rain till then."

"Rain before seven, fine before eleven," repeated Gramma maddeningly, and Lizzie went to the window and stared out, and thought: "*Could* rain all day—'course it could. Forty days and forty nights, it could, if it felt like it. . . !

Lizzie could see the church tower from where she stood, and seeing it she thought of the graveyard, and then—the witch.

"What if . . . I wonder if . . . no. . . . Worth trying, though. If it hasn't stopped raining by . . . by half-past ten, I'll go. No harm. . . ."

It had not stopped raining by half-past ten, and Lizzie accordingly put on her anorak and went out. Toby, in sou'wester and oilskins, was making mud pies. Lizzie edged past him and went up Church Lane and over Kirk Street and into the churchyard. When she went through the iron gate she hesitated a little. The graveyard was dank and dripping. It was full of unaccustomed stir and sound, and yet, curiously, more empty and alone than it had ever seemed under the sun.

Lizzie had not for one moment imagined that the witch would be sitting, intrepid, on the tomb of the Perfectly Peaceful Posts knitting her wet wool, oblivious of the steadily falling rain. She was not even certain that the witch would materialise in the rain even if Lizzie called her.

"After all," she thought, "if she comes visible, she'll get wet. I expect she's dry, *invisible*."

She thought of something else, too. Lately, the witch had become less and less predictable. Often she would not appear at all, and even on the days when she did, would hardly have a word for Lizzie. She just sat there, counting stitches under her breath and sulking.

"Witch!" called Lizzie, and the word seemed to hang forlornly for an instant in the drift of rain. She called again: "Witch! It's me—Lizzie!"

She felt ridiculous, standing there wet and alone, talking to herself, it seemed.

"No good," she thought. "Might've known."

She turned and walked slowly back past the dripping laurels by the side of the church, and as she did so heard the witch's voice, mirthful and infuriating: "Rain before seven, fine before eleven!"

Lizzie whirled about. "Witch?"

She paused only an instant before going on again. She was not in the mood for games of hide and seek. Just as she put her hand on the wet, cold metal of the little gate, she heard it again: "Rain before seven, fine before eleven!" and a long, fading cackle of laughter.

Lizzie marched on. As she passed the Memorial Hall she looked up at the poster she and Jonathan had made and saw that the colours were beginning to run. She crossed the road, and as

she did so the church clock began to strike eleven. Head down, she kicked a stone all the way home and stamped in puddles. She went past Toby, muddy and red-cheeked in the border, and into the living-room where Patty was cutting bread.

"There you are!" cried Gramma triumphantly. "What did I tell you!"

"What?" Lizzie was tugging at her wellingtons.

"Rain before seven, fine before eleven!"

"But—but it hasn't, it—"

Lizzie, right by the door still, threw it open.

"It has!"

And she had not even noticed, eyes glued on the ground, kicking stones through puddles.

"Hurray!" she shouted. "And sun's coming through—it is—see it, behind the church!"

At two o'clock Lizzie was by the milk table by Stokes's farm, which was the starting point, helping Miss Platt give out cards.

There was one between each family, and each party was sent off at two-minute intervals. Gram took a card.

"Don't know half the clues," she said. "*Heard* 'em enough times, but not to know 'em."

Lizzie pulled at Albert's sleeve.

"Eeeeh—look! Mam, look! It's them!"

Coming up Main Street laden with carrier bags and unmistakably headed for the Treasure Hunt, were Jack Jackson and family.

"Oh my good gracious!" exclaimed Patty.

"Steady on, pair of you," said Albert evenly. "Nothing amiss in that. Afternoon, Jack. Afternoon Irma. And how's Steven? Going to win the Treasure Hunt, are you?"

"Yes," said Steven eagerly. "Dad and Mam've won a hunt before, only in a car. Dad's laid me five to one we'll win!"

"Aye, well—you've won then, young 'un, whatever happens," said Albert. "Covered both ways, as they say."

"It's to be hoped grass isn't still damp, for the picnic," said Irma. "Not really my cup of tea, picnics. But there you are. They would come."

"Here we are, then, Mr Jackson," said Miss Platt. "This is yours. You'll notice you have to collect various items as you go along, before you give in the card at the end."

Then the Jackson family were off at a fast walk to follow the first clue and to walk, eventually, through their own lettuces.

"Can *we* go next, Miss Platt," cried Lizzie. "I could go along with Gram—I'd not help her, honest, and we'd not take the prize even if we won it. Dad and Mam're going straight there, to take Toby, but I'd like to go on the trail!"

"Very well, Lizzie," said Miss Platt. "I can manage now, thank you."

Lizzie and Gramma set off.

"Let's miss the first three clues out," said Lizzie, once they were out of earshot. "Then we could take the short cut up jitty and see his face when he gets to his lettuces."

"No, I shan't do that," said Gramma righteously. "Matter of

principle this is, Lizzie, and no need for any o' that."

"Well *I* shall," thought Lizzie rebelliously. "I shall hide behind the hedge and *watch* 'em."

And so she did. By the time Jack Jackson reached the lettuce patch Gramma was away over the field towards Pulpit Ash, a lone black figure on the green, and a public footpath was already beginning to take shape again among the lettuces. (Gramma, true to her word, had stamped on several, and Lizzie, close behind, had followed suit.)

The Jacksons came to a halt and Lizzie could see a scowl on Jack's face, a considerable one, even from that distance.

"Oooh, Jack, your lettuces!" She heard Irma's scream. "Oooh—I told you not to do that, I did, and now look!"

"I see," said Jack ominously, once he had taken things in. "Come on now, quick—fast, pair on you! Win this I will now, or bust!" and the Jacksons came steaming through their own lettuces so fast that Lizzie barely had time to creep round the hedge out of their sight.

Lizzie ran a different way then to rejoin Gramma by Pulpit Ash. After that, Gramma gave up the hunt too, and she and Lizzie took another short cut, to Hell Hills where the picnic was to be. Albert and Patty and several others were already there. Toby was roly-polying on the slope with squeals of delight. Lizzie ran to him and gave him little pushes till faster and faster he went, tumbling right to the very bottom, a chuckling, red-faced bundle.

"Oooh, smashing . . ." Lizzie lay on her back and sniffed the smell of clover made strong by rain with hot sun following. Jonathan came whirling down too, and after a while they went back up and rolled down again, racing.

"Smashing old hill, this," Lizzie told him. "Should see us sledding down it, in winter. Hey, does your Aunt Blodwen *let* you roll down hills?" Jonathan tore up handfuls of grass and flowers and pelted Lizzie with them, and she ducked away, squealing.

The food came next. The Arbuckles had sausage rolls, ham and egg sandwiches, chocolate cake and apples—and almost anything else you could think of, because what Lizzie didn't have she could always swap for with someone else.

Then Miss Platt stood up to announce the winners.

"First prize goes to the one who followed the trail correctly," she said, "brought all the items asked for, and lastly, found five different kinds of wild flower here on Hell Hills. And that prize," she paused, "goes to—Jack Jackson and family!"

"Well dang me!" cried Gramma, regardless of the Jacksons who were sitting only a few yards away. The people of Little Hemlock, who knew a joke when they saw one, cheered and yelled as Jack went up to take his prize. Each and every one of them had trampled through Jack Jackson's lettuce patch, so it was really a kind of poetic justice.

Jack took his prize, a long cardboard roll, and started back to his place.

"What's in it, Lizzie?" whispered Patty, and Lizzie shook her head.

"Don't know, Mam. Miss Platt gave it."

"Well fair does," said Albert, and clapped with the rest. As Jack came back to his place he shot a triumphant look towards the Arbuckles.

"Well done, Jack," said Albert. "What've you got there, then?"

"Yes, go on, Jack, open it up," cried Irma fussily. "My word, fancy our winning!"

"Aye, fancy!" Lizzie heard Gramma mutter, and turned aside her own face to hide a smile. Jack put his fingers in the end of the roll and drew out a paper.

"A picture!" cried Irma. "That's what it is!"

Jack unrolled it and stared blankly for a moment. Albert went round behind and looked over his shoulder.

"Map!" said Jack at last.

"Aye," said Albert, straight faced, "be a lot of use will that, Jack. Ordnance Survey, large scale, see, of Little Hemlock. Every last field, hedge, ditch and footpath on there."

And Albert winked, very deliberately, at Lizzie and

Gramma, and Jack, over the top of his map, glared at the inno-
cent Arbuckles and Lizzie thought, "Oooh—we won, after all!"

And she did not wait even to hear the other prizes, she threw
herself into another mad roly-poly. The grass, the shouting, the
clover and the sky whirled together in her head and she
thought, "Oooh, what a perfect day!" and could hardly contain
her happiness. Because perfect days, as Lizzie well knew, don't
grow on trees.

Lizzie Dripping
by the Sea

"Oooh Dad!" squealed Lizzie Dripping. "Smashing!"

"What, just like that?" cried Patty. "Up and off without a minute's notice?"

"I reckon that's the way to do it," said Albert. "Run up on it while it ain't looking, like. Ages since we last had sniff of the sea."

"Cough cough cough all winter, I was." Gramma said, and coughed hard now to illustrate it. "Need a sniff of sea, I do."

"Well, I've eggs, of course," said Patty dubiously, taking mental stock of her larder. "And I can always open a tin of salmon, and there's—"

"Look, Patty love," said Albert, "give over, will you? We shall go to a cafe."

"A cafe?" cried Patty. "Just hark at him! But the price, Albert!"

"You never mind about price. We shall get up at six, set off for Yarbury and have our dinners at a cafe—one of them along sea front."

"Oooh, it would be nice," said Patty. "Always put in a few hard-boiled eggs, and that, to fill us."

"Can Jonathan go?" asked Lizzie then. "Told him I'd play tomorrow. And he'd like it."

"So long as that scrubby little aunt of his don't come," put in Gramma.

Patty and Albert exchanged looks.

"She'll have to be *usked*, Ma," said Patty. "And she is my friend, you know."

"She'll not go," put in Lizzie. "Not tidy enough, seaside ain't, not for her."

"And that'll do from you, miss," said Patty.

"Don't see how she can go, anyhow," Lizzie muttered. "There'll be no room, not for all them people."

"Aye, well, you see," said Albert. "I've fixed up with Bill Larkin to borrow his car. Swap, like, for the day."

"Oooh, we have got things off pat, haven't we," cried Patty, excited again. "You nip off down to Blodwen's now, Lizzie, and see if they'll come. Six o'clock, tell them, and we'll pick them up."

Lizzie was through the door in a moment and heard Patty's voice after her: "And not to bother with sandwiches, tell her. Tell her we shall go to a cafe."

"Wheee!" Lizzie sped down the garden path and could smell, even in the midst of her excitement, the strong night smell of lavender and stock and drying grass. There in the road, in place of Albert's old van, was Bill Larkin's estate car, big and shining.

"Oooh—it's all true, then!" and Lizzie pelted on.

At the corner of Church Lane, on an impulse, she ran straight over the road and up along the side of the church and took the short cut into the graveyard. She stood panting long enough to see that the witch was not there disguised as a black shadow in the low evening sunlight. Then she cupped her hands to her mouth and yelled, "Not coming tomorrow, witch! Sorry—can't. Going to the seaside! Tara, witch!"

And giving the witch not the blink of an eye in which to reply she was off again, through the rich gold of the evening, to tell the news to Aunt Blodwen and Jonathan.

Lizzie was awake at dawn when the birds were whistling and a faint milky haze over the hills of Mapleburn promised a day of glorious heat. The Arbuckles packed their belongings into the car and set off.

"You'd think we was going for a week, all this stuff!" cried Patty. She settled luxuriously into her seat beside Albert. "Oooh, lovely car this is, feel like a queen, don't you?"

"Get yourself killed in any car," said Gramma. "And a little 'un'll do it as good as a big 'un."

"Eh up, Albert," cried Patty, "right, here, remember. Blodwen yet."

"And my luck to get sat next to her," said Gramma sourly. She peered out the window as Albert drew up outside Blodwen's trim little house. Lizzie saw the net curtains at the window twitch and next minute Aunt Blodwen came out, with Jonathan following.

"Well!" exclaimed Gramma. "Dolled up like the dog's dinner! Just you look at that! Reckons she's going to Buckingham Palace, that one does!"

"Sssh, Ma!" hissed Patty.

"And look at him!" cried Lizzie. "Oh Mam, she'll never let him play on beach!"

"Sssh!" hissed Patty again, and wound down her window.

"Next Gramma, Blodwen," she said. "And Jonathan in the back with Lizzie and Toby."

Gramma shuffled ungraciously across the back seat so that she was sitting at the extreme far side, right against the door.

"My word," said Aunt Blodwen as Albert drove off. "Posh we are, today. Lovely car, Albert."

She snuggled fussily into her corner and Lizzie in the back made faces at Jonathan and pointed at his clothes and he in turn made faces at Aunt Blodwen's back and pointed at *her*.

"Lovely day, by the look of it," went on Aunt Blodwen. "It's to be hoped Yarbury won't be full of day trippers. Lowers the tone of a place, day trippers, I always think."

Gramma, a mint imperial poised at her lips, spoke up then from her corner. "*We're* only going for the day," she said.

"Oh!" Aunt Blodwen gave a light little laugh. "Not like *us* for heaven's sake! *Real* day trippers, that's what I meant, see—eating chips out of paper bags and kids screaming . . . snagging your tights with their buckets and spades!"

She shuddered, and no one spoke for a moment. Then Albert struck up, "I do like to be beside the seaside!"

"I do like to be beside the sea . . ." chorused Patty and Lizzie.

And after that they rollicked along as all the best day trippers do, while Aunt Blodwen pursed her lips and smoothed her skirts and made it perfectly plain that she was wishing, already, that she had never come.

By nine o'clock the Arbuckles were at Yarbury and the first things they saw were big posters, and banners hung across the streets. As soon as Albert drew the car up in the park on the front Lizzie got out and ran over to read one of the posters.

"Yarbury Carnival Week, June the third to the tenth. Oooh, that's today!" she cried. "It's seventh today, and look, Mam, fancy dress parade at two-thirty! Oh—I wish I'd known—could've dressed up!"

"Pity we didn't check before we started," said Aunt Blodwen. "Day trippers galore, I shouldn't wonder."

"Get down to beach, shall we?" suggested Albert.

"Oooh yes!" cried Lizzie. And the moment she saw the sea her legs seemed to go wild with excitement of their own accord, and she jumped off the promenade onto the sand and ran in wide, giddy circles, laughing and shrieking. At last she collapsed, dizzy and breathless, and lay with her eyes shut and listened to the gulls and the falling waves and thought for a moment that she actually felt the world stop turning, and time standing still. She put out her hand and felt the cool sand trickle between her fingers and thought, "I can hear the sea, right through the sand. . . . I feel like a sea shell. Wouldn't mind being a sea shell . . . one of them curly ones. . . ."

She sat up there and looked about for the others. They were still standing where she had left them, and it looked as if they were having an argument.

"Aunt Blodwen, I s'pose," she thought, and got up. "Spoil everything, she will." And she climbed up again and joined them.

"Well, you know best, Blodwen," Patty was saying, in a voice that said the exact opposite. "If it's shops you've come to see, you go an *look* at shops."

"No harm *Jonathan* going on beach," said Aunt Blodwen, "so long as he behaves himself and keeps himself clean."

Lizzie said the last words to herself, in chorus with Aunt Blodwen.

"See you in cafe then, shall we?" said Albert. "Lobster Pot at one o' clock."

"And you behave yourself, Jonathan," said Aunt Blodwen, "and do as you're told, and mind you keep yourself clean."

Again Lizzie mouthed the words in unison and she pulled a face after Aunt Blodwen's retreating back.

"Good riddance," she whispered to Jonathan, and he nodded.

"That's her out way, then," remarked Gramma cheerfully. "On beach shall we, Albert? Get us deckchairs put up?"

The Arbuckles accordingly staked their claim on Yarbury beach. A windbreak was put up, after a great deal of argument as to which way the wind was blowing, and Toby was given a bucket and spade.

"That'll settle him, for the morning," observed Patty. Gramma took out her knitting.

"Oh, Gram!" cried Lizzie. "You're never going to knit!"

"And why not?" enquired Gramma. "Not one for idling, me, seaside or no."

"But you can knit at home!" Lizzie persisted. "Come and paddle—go on, Gram, do!"

"I never in this world shall!" retorted Gramma. "Legs like I've got, and paddle?"

"You will, Mam, won't you," pleaded Lizzie.

"And Dad?"

"Have a bit of a dabble later, I might," said Albert. "You and

Jonathan run down, eh, and let me know what water's like?"

He had rolled up his shirt sleeves and his trouser legs, and now sat back in his deckchair and began to light his pipe.

"Dratted pattern," muttered Gramma. "Which way's out? Can't tell which from which. . . !"

"Witch from witch . . ." Lizzie caught the words and translated them.

"Witch . . ." she thought. "Funny . . . can't hardly believe in her, not here . . . Wonder if she heard what I said last night. Wonder if she's waiting. . . ?"

And no sooner had the thought dissolved than she thought she saw, for the merest fraction of a minute, a raggedy black shape away on the tideline, a pointed hat. Lizzie gasped, shut her eyes and shook her head hard to settle her brains.

"Oooh look!" shrieked Patty, and Lizzie, startled, jerked up, her eyes wide open again.

"By heck!" said Gramma. "A bear!"

"And a witch!" cried Patty. "Look, Lizzie! Look, Toby—bear!"

"Bear!" repeated Toby, wide-eyed.

Lizzie, very slowly, turned her head, prepared for the worst. Strolling along Yarbury sands arm in arm were, indeed, a bear and a witch. Lizzie shut her eyes again quickly.

"Oh—what's she doing?" she thought desperately. "Oooh—she's *followed* me! What'll I *do*?"

"Here Albert!" She heard Patty's voice. "Get camera—look sharp!"

Lizzie opened her eyes again. The witch was right near-by now.

"*Not* her!" She actually said the words out loud, so enormous, so overwhelming was her relief.

"You what?" said Patty absently. "Come on, Albert, you'll miss them!"

"Don't look owt like a witch!" thought Lizzie scornfully. "Proper fancy dress witch she is—don't she *know* what a real witch looks like?"

The witch in question was about ten years old. She wore a false nose on a band of elastic, had fair hair tangled among the grey wool that sprouted from under her hat, and brown sandals and white socks were clearly visible beneath her cloak. Also, her eyes were blue.

"Take a picture, can I?" asked Albert.

"All right!" came a high, unwitchlike voice. A hand came out from under the cloak and poked the bear in the middle. "Stand *still* Mark, will you, the man wants to take our pictures."

The bear and the witch both stood stiffly to attention and Albert clicked the camera.

"Ta!" he said. "In for the fancy dress, are you?"

The bear nodded.

"It's hot in here," came a muffled voice.

"Aye, well, have to take your head off and cool down," said

93

Albert. "Have to take your head off for your dinner anyhow, shan't you?"

The bear nodded again.

"It's all right him talking," said the witch. "My *nose* hurts. I *told* Mam it'd hurt."

"Best take nose off then, an' all," suggested Albert. "Not till this afternoon is it, parade?"

"Here, look," said the witch, pulling at the bear's slack fur, "there's that stupid Susan Coombes coming, all got up in a sheet! Come on, Mark, quick, before she sees us!"

The bear and the witch moved smartly off and the Arbuckles turned to see three other apparitions strolling towards them.

"Don't it seem queer, though?" cried Patty. "Never seen sights like *this* on the beach afore. Ghost, look—and what's she. . . ?"

Lizzie did not hear the rest, because all of a sudden it seemed that the gulls were shrieking and flying in storm as if panicked. And mingled with their cries she thought she heard the coarse, unmistakable cackle of a witch, so she looked back towards the sea and saw, quite distinctly, the witch again, on the tideline, like some impossible flotsam.

"Let's go and paddle!" she heard Jonathan say. "Come on, Lizzie!"

She thought rapidly.

"I know!" she cried "You go that way!" and she pointed wildly, away from the witch. "And I'll go the other, and first—first to find a crab shell buys the other an ice lolly!"

"Right!" said Jonathan. "First back here with a crab shell!" and he was off, spurting sand.

"That's him out way," thought Lizzie. "Now. . . ."

And she began to walk steadily towards the witch, keeping her eyes fixed on her.

"One thing," she thought, "won't matter if they *do* see her, not here. Think she's a fancy dress witch, they will. . . ."

"Hee hee!" She heard the witch's cackle, oddly camouflaged today because of the squawking of the gulls.

The witch was paddling, skirts held up, more impossible now than she had ever seemed in Little Hemlock, among the gravestones. Lizzie stopped and stared at her.

"Hee!" cried the witch. "I like it, I do! Better than knitting! Hee!"

"But you shouldn't've come!" cried Lizzie. "You shouldn't've!"

The witch turned on her, her eyes flashing green sparks.

"And why not?" she snapped. "Anywhere you go, *I* can go, girl, remember that! Anywhere!"

"Oh I know—I know that," said poor Lizzie. "But what if—what if Mam and Dad was to see you, or Jonathan?"

The witch cackled merrily and did not answer. She kicked her skinny feet in the water and made herself a halo of spray.

"Lucky for you there's a fancy dress," said Lizzie. "Lucky for

me, and all. One thing, anyhow. Don't believe in witches, Jonathan don't. Told me so."

"Don't—*what*?"

The witch advanced out of the sea and was all at once menacing again, a witch-on-holiday changed to a witch-on-business in the blink of an eye.

"*Everyone* don't, you know!" said Lizzie desperately. "It's not just him!"

"Hmmmm . . ."

The witch was looking past Lizzie at something beyond, and turning, Lizzie saw Jonathan approaching, holding something aloft on the end of a stick.

"Got one!" she heard his faint cry. "I've won!"

"Not toads . . ." the witch was murmuring, "don't fit, toads at sea. Crab! That's it! Turn crab. . . ."

"Oh, you—oh, not him!" cried Lizzie aghast. "He's got an Auntie Blodwen, and she'd kill me!"

But the witch was already raising her skinny hands and Jonathan was coming nearer every moment, blissfully unaware that crabhood was only a pincer's breadth away.

"Now!" cried the witch.

Lizzie shut her eyes. She heard the scream of gulls, the crash of waves, and Jonathan's voice, oddly blurred and far away: "Lizzie! Come on—what's up?"

Lizzie opened her eyes and was looking down at the wet sand strewn with weeds and stones. There, right by her foot, was a large crab—a live crab.

She screamed then. She screamed loudly and madly and felt herself being shaken and looked up to see Jonathan's face only a few inches off her own and screamed again, one last scream.

"It's only a crab!" he cried.

"I thought—I thought—" stammered Lizzie. She looked down. The crab was still there. She looked at where the witch was and saw that the witch was not, and wondered fleetingly whether it was *herself* she had changed into a crab.

"Trust a girl to be afraid of a crab," said Jonathan, and began to walk off. "Anyhow, we didn't say a live crab, so I've still won, and I'll have an orange whopper, thanks."

Lizzie glared after him, then followed.

"Orange whopper's what you'd've been," she thought, "if she'd've done that spell, and you ended up on a slab . . ."

"Well!" said Patty as they stepped outside again into the cold, sea-smelling air. "That was a yarking good meal, Albert, whatever *she* says!" (With a jerk of the head towards Gramma.) "I'm that full I can hardly stir."

"I don't say owt about food," said Gramma. "Food was all right. What I'm saying is, I can't abide my dinner off a pink

97

plate. For cakes, pink plates is, and don't go with roast and greens at all. Particular carrots. Nasty, carrots is, off pink plates."

"Oh shush up, Ma, do, about pink plates!" cried Patty. "Now what about this here fancy dress? Watch that, shall us, while our dinners go down?"

"Not me, Patty, if you don't mind," said Blodwen.

"Go to the Bingo shall you, then?" asked Patty.

"Oh!" Aunt Blodwen gave her light, superior Welsh laugh. "No, thank you, Patty."

"I shall go down Bingo later on," announced Gramma. She popped in a mint imperial, and poked her tongue about among her teeth. "I could do with some new teeth, you know."

Blodwen shuddered delicately.

"Meet you at car park shall I then?" she said. "Six o' clock, is it?"

"We shan't go without you, Blodwen," said Albert.

"More's the pity!" thought Lizzie.

But Blodwen out of sight was quickly forgotten, and by the time the Arbuckles had stationed themselves on the beach the fancy dress parade was about to begin.

"There's that bear!" cried Jonathan. "Look, Mr Arbuckle, the one you took picture of!"

"And there's the witch!" cried Patty.

Lizzie looked and saw the bear and the witch. Behind them she saw something else.

"Oh no!" she cried inwardly.

Walking behind Humpty Dumpty and in front of Little Bo Peep was the witch. She was smiling happily and making exaggerated bows and waves on either hand, as if the applause in Yarbury were meant for her alone.

"One thing," thought Lizzie, "she'll not win. Can't. There's two witches, and they can't both win the prize!"

She looked sideways at the faces of the those nearest to her for signs that they had realised that this was a real witch they were looking at, but they were cheering and clapping and pointing and taking photographs in the most ordinary way possible. You might almost have thought they did not see the witch at all, Lizzie thought, so obvious did it seem to her that this was no fancy dress witch, but a real, live, spelling, toad-turning witch, who lived in a graveyard and could turn the world upside down if she wanted.

The witch looked straight into Lizzie's eyes then and grinned wickedly. Lizzie shook her head and frowned, but the witch stretched up a thin hand, snapped her fingers, and a bunch of balloons was all at once there, like bubbles bursting into the air. Lizzie gasped. Now, surely, someone would point a finger and shout,

"Look out! A witch! Beware!"

But no one did, and the witch went by and out of sight and by the time Lizzie had collected herself a voice was coming over the loudspeakers.

"Fancy dress competitors will now assemble on foot in front of the judges for the final line-up. Our judges will be Alderman J. Cornforth, Mayor of Yarbury, and a visitor to the town, selected at random only a few minutes ago on the promenade. Would you mind telling us your name, madam?"

"Cole," came a familiar voice. "Mrs Blodwen Cole, from Little Hemlock."

"Oooh!" shrieked Patty.

"Well I'll go to the foot of our stairs!" ejaculated Albert, removing his pipe from his mouth for the purpose.

"Her?" cried Gramma. "Judge?"

"Mrs Blodwen Cole has sportingly agreed to come along here and help our Mayor to decide on the winners," came the voice, "so shall we all give her a round of applause?"

"*I* ain't clapping," said Gramma disgustedly. "*I'd've* done it if

I'd known they was a judge short."

"There'll be no holding her now," said Patty.

The fancy dress competitors were walking round in a circle now beneath the promenade where the judges sat. The witch was still there. She was simply standing in the middle while the others walked round her, as if she were playing "Poor Mary sat a-weeping."

"Oooh, what's she doing?" thought Lizzie desperately. "She thinks she's won! Oooh, what'll she do when she finds she ain't? Doing this to spite me, she is."

There was a renewed burst of applause and Lizzie saw that the Mayor was on his feet now, paper in hand, while Aunt Blodwen sat smirking beside him.

"Ladies and Gentlemen," he said, "—and children, of course—I and my charming co-judge," he bowed towards Aunt Blodwen who smirked the more and wriggled in her seat, "have unanimously decided on the winners. And first prize," he paused, "first prize goes to—the snail!"

A snail was pushed forward by the rest and moved up to the judge at a very un-snail-like pace. The judge wanted to shake hands and give the prize, but both the snail's hands were under its shell, so it stood there, quite helplessly, shaking its horns while the crowd laughed and cheered.

But what Lizzie saw was the witch's face, scowling and vengeful and her hands lifted, poised for spelling.

"Oooh—can't they see she's real?" thought Lizzie. "She'll have 'em all into seagulls! Ooh, let her have second prize, let her!"

But the judge was already announcing the second prize, and a Welsh lady with a conical witch's hat came mincing forward. Aunt Blodwen preened, the witch drew herself into a taut hunch of fury. A swift shake of the fist and a poisonous darting look at Aunt Blodwen and—she was gone!

Lizzie let out her breath.

"Thank goodness! But oh dear, she'll not've gone for good.

Get her own back, that witch will, before she's done. What'll she *do*, though. . . ? *Something* awful. . . ."

"Giddy you get, doing this . . ." Lizzie stood ankle-deep and watched the water rushing up and then ebbing back, brown with a soft draining of sand and shingle and a pulling and falling away of the sand beneath her feet.

"Wish I lived at the sea . . . might do, when I grow up. Have one of them little kiosk things, up the pier. . . ."

She looked towards the pier. There was the witch, leaning on the white rails.

"Oh!" Lizzie's hand flew up to her mouth. The witch melted into air and became in the instant twice as alarming.

"Now where's she gone? Hanging over the place like a—like a blessed vulture! Trying to pay me out, I s'pose, for not going to the graveyard. But I *can't* every day—told her that before. She should never've made me promise!"

The seagulls screeched noisily close at hand and Lizzie jumped nervously and watched them, almost expecting to see the witch in flight among them. And she could hear a voice in the clamour: "Them that breaks a promise, pays a forfeit!"

Lizzie turned her back on pier and gulls alike, and paddled back along the creaming frill of the tide, savouring the cold salt on her feet and in her nostrils, but still, despite it all, she could not forget that witch.

"Funny thing is, how did she get here? How did she know where I was—never *told* her?"

A few waves later the thought occurred, "To do with *me*, that witch is. I thought she was to do with the graveyard, mainly. But it's not. It's me. . . ."

She pondered the matter for the break of another wave or two.

"Does anyone else see her, besides me? Anyone else in the whole world . . . ? Is she *my* witch, *really* mine . . . ? Ask the others. . . ."

So she left the sea and went back to the rest of the Arbuckles who were burying Albert. He lay there like an effigy with a live flesh face. Even his face was whiskered with sand, and so comical that Lizzie forgot her question and found herself laughing and kneeling with the others to scoop sand over him.

"Steady!" said Albert. "Live to tell the tale, I should like to."

"If we covered your face now," said Jonathan, "you'd be dead. Dead and buried."

"Oh charming!" cried Patty. "Hear that, Albert?"

"Didn't say I would," said Jonathan. "But if I did, he would."

"*And* no joke," put in Gramma. "At seaside and talking about dead! Be quiet about dead, will you! And keep yourself clean, my lad, if you don't want that aunt of yours round your backside."

Albert raised himself up onto his elbows then and the sand crumpled and fell away and the game was over.

"Mam," said Lizzie, remembering, "did you see that witch?"

"Witch?" Patty was peeling a banana and only half listening.

"There was a witch with that bear," said Jonathan. "Your dad took a picture."

"Another witch, I mean," persisted Lizzie.

"Swarming with them, this place is," said Patty. "Bears, witches, frogs—never seen the like. That one"—(with a jerk of the head towards Toby) "—'ll about grow *up* thinking there's bears and frogs at seaside!"

"But a real one—*looking* real, I mean. Not fancy dress."

"Oh yes!" said Patty, sarcastic now. "In the sky, you mean, on a broomstick?"

"Or invisible," suggested Jonathan innocently. "I saw an *invisible* witch."

Lizzie gritted her teeth hard.

"I just wish," she thought, "I'd *let* her turn you into a crab now. I wish you'd been made crab, boiled, and we'd all *ate* you, in sandwiches, with cress!"

"Tide's coming up fast," said Albert, who specialised in changing the subject if the occasion seemed to demand it. "Best start moving things up."

103

"Oooh!" cried Patty. "It *has* come up in a rush! Come along Lizzie, help get these things together, will you. And you'd best budge fast, Ma, if you don't want to get swept out to sea."

Gramma did not budge.

"*That* one'll get swept out to sea," she remarked, nodding. The Arbuckles all turned. The sea had swept in to fill a low wide dip and had left a spit of sand beyond still uncovered. On it was a solitary figure in a deckchair, facing out to sea, oblivious of the fact that she was already marooned.

"By heck!" said Albert. "*She'll* get her feet wet. Best give her a shout. Fallen off to sleep, likely, and not noticed."

He went forward, followed by the others, cupping his hands as he went and shouting: "Ahoy! Look out! Tide's coming! Ahoy!"

At the same time the deckchair boy came scooting down the beach in a spurt of sand, yelling and waving. "My chair that is!" he cried. "Corporation chair she's sitting on!"

He went splashing straight into the water and waded over, up to his knees. As he approached the figure in the deckchair rose and turned and let out a shrill scream. Albert and the others stood transfixed.

"It's Blodwen!" squealed Patty. "Oh—she'll be drownded!"

"Help!" screamed Blodwen and lurched to the water's edge where she stood helplessly. The deckchair boy, ignoring her, grabbed up the chair and made back with it, splashing in again and sending a shower of spray right over Aunt Blodwen making her look, for a second, almost romantic.

"You want to watch it, missis!" they heard his voice. "Paid for this, I should've had to, out my wages, if you'd been swept off!"

Back he threshed, deckchair in tow. Aunt Blodwen bent and began to tear off her shoes and stockings and Lizzie, hand over her mouth now to hide the laughter that came irresistibly surging up, thought: "The witch! It's her doing, all right! Witch's revenge!"

"And mind you keep yourself clean!" she heard Jonathan splutter behind her. They all stood and watched while aunt

104

Blodwen, shoes and stockings held aloft, hat awry and water up above her skirts now, waded for safety.

"She *will* create!" Patty said.

"Her *turn* to get wet, I reckon," observed Gramma calmly behind them, and Blodwen moaned and squealed and lurched and all at once the day was made perfect—absolutely and beautifully, poetically perfect.

Lizzie Dripping
Says Goodbye

"Growing up now, you are, our Lizzie," Patty said. "Though sometimes I wonder if you ever will. And time you come down to earth a bit, never mind always off mooning about in graveyards."

"Not always," said Lizzie sulkily. "What's it to do with old Ma Bates, anyhow?"

"Nowt at all to do," said Gramma with asperity. "Wants to mind her own business, that one does. Not keeper of the graveyard, she's not, for owt I know."

"Not the point, Ma," said Patty. "Just mentioned it to me, that's all. *See* graveyard, she can, from her house."

"And good job she never saw *witch*," Lizzie thought.

"Not nice, anyhow," Patty went on. "Going off to play in graveyards. Concentrated ground that is, Lizzie. Show some respect for the dead, you're meant to, in them sort of places."

"Dead'll not mind," observed Gramma with conviction. "It's Ma Bates as minds, not dead."

"Anyhow, you keep off from there, Lizzie," Patty said. "D'you hear? Plenty of other places to play, besides graveyards."

"I don't play, Mam," Lizzie told her. "I—I think and that."

"Oh! Think, is it?" cried Patty. "Nice cheerful thoughts you'll get there, I'll be bound! Downright morbid it is, a girl of your age. I don't know where you get it from, I don't really."

Lizzie said nothing.

106

"And what're you going to do with yourself today?" Patty asked. "Because if you—"

"Project," said Lizzie quickly. "Holiday project."

"Oooh. Never had them sorts of thing in my day," said Patty. "Not that I'm grumbling, mind. Keeps you out the road, anyhow. What is it you're doing this time, then?"

"Oooh, it's ever so good! Miss Platt's idea it was. What we're doing, see, is making a record of Little Hemlock, for posterity."

"Posterity!" Patty threw up her hands. "Lawks—whatever next!"

"We're doing everything about what it's like to be alive in 1990, see," explained Lizzie. "Then it's to be put in a tin box, and locked, and given parson to keep with the parish records, Miss Platt says. And on it it'll say *Not to be opened till 2090*. We'll all be dead then. Even *I'll* be dead, let alone you."

"Charming," said Patty. "Here we go again. Back to the graveyard. I begin to think you'll not be happy till you're buried."

"Then posterity'll know what it was like now, see," said Lizzie. "Posterity's the opposite of ancestors, you know. It means people who live *after* you."

"What sort of things you putting in?" enquired Gramma. "You putting in price of things? You want to put price of things, Lizzie. That'll give 'em summat to think about. You put price of eggs—*and* a loaf! By heck, *that'll* give 'em summat to think about!"

"We ain't just doing things like that, Gram," Lizzie told her. "Though we are doing it, and putting in things like newspapers, and that—*Radio Times*. But we're doing about people as well, see. All got five each to interview, like. And we're to do our own families, and all. And Miss Platt said grandparents were very important. To ask them specially, she said."

"Did she, now," said Gramma, pleased, and shot Patty a triumphant look.

"Yes. 'Cos they can remember further back, see. So when they open box in 2090 they'll know what it was like nearly *two* hundred years ago, let alone one!"

"Here, steady on," said Gramma. "Not a hundred I'm not, thank you. Remember when bread was a penny a loaf I can, though."

"That's kind of thing," Lizzie nodded. "And we're doing countryside as well—map on it, with all hedges and trees and footpaths marked. And wild flowers—all got a field each to do, and we're to pick flowers, see, and press them, and—"

"Flowers?" interrupted Patty. "Flowers'll be same in a hundred years as they are now." she laughed. "Daisies look same to me now as they did when I was a kid, any road."

"But there might not *be* any daisies," said Lizzie, half enjoying the drama of such a statement, half horrorstruck at the very idea of its possibly being true.

Patty stared at her, then laughed again, evidently having

decided it could not be true.

"It's true! Miss Platt says it's all the spraying and that. She says if any of us find a hedgerow with more than fourteen kinds of wild flower in it, we're to tell her, and she'll have it preserved."

"Preserved?" echoed Patty. To her, things that were preserved were in bottles, like greengage jam. And she could not picture a bottled hedgerow, quite.

"Kept," explained Lizzie. "Protected, like. Nobody let go spraying it, and that. Jonathan's helping me. Not that he's much help. Hardly knows a celandine from a buttercup, he doesn't. . . ."

Jonathan sprawled in the long hot grass while Lizzie herself was kneeling in it. She examined the clover carefully, because what she really wanted was a four-leafed one. The sun burned into her skin, the cuckoo called and Lizzie thought: "Wish I could put today in the tin box with a label on it: 'July 14th, 1990'. Wish I could put the whole thing in—sun, cuckoo, smells and all."

Unconsciously she stretched out her arms in a vain attempt to draw the whole thing together, embrace it. The woods on the skyline shimmered in the heat and Lizzie could even imagine the coolness inside there in the green light under the trees and the ker-ker of comfortable, well-fed pigeons and the drone of summer flies in ferns.

"Could take a *photo*, I s'pose," she thought. "That might do it."

She took the polaroid camera she had been given last Christmas and peered through the lens, trying to find the view that would tell best how it had been on this particular summer day in 1990. Lizzie heard the shutter click, withdrew the film and tucked it under her arm while it developed.

A minute later she was looking at it, and knew at once that she had failed. The view was there, right enough, but something was missing, some all-important quality whose absence made

109

the photograph a mere—photograph. Lizzie sighed.

"Pity," she murmured aloud.

"What?" Jonathan's eyes were closed and he was sucking at a long grass.

"Pity you can't put *real* things in a box to keep. I mean, it's all right putting price of eggs, and how Gramma won Sunday School prize when she was little. But when they open it, in 2090, I don't reckon it'll *tell* 'em anything. Not really."

"So what do you want to put in?" enquired Jonathan, eyes still shut. "A piece of birthday cake?"

Lizzie looked down at him.

"Not a bad idea, that's not," she told him. Then she looked back at the landscape spellbound in the heat.

"Today. That's what I'd put in if I could. How it *feels*."

Jonathan opened his eyes, squinting into the sun.

"They'll still have days like this," he said. "Bound to, even in 2090."

"Not exactly," said Lizzie, certain of it. "Never be a day again *exactly* like today. Even we'll never have one exactly the same. 'Cos *we'll* be different, see."

"Oh, well!" Jonathan spat out the grass, picked another, then lay back and shut his eyes again. "Wish we could get done with the wild flowers and get on with the *interviewing*. I'm going to do Aunt Blodwen."

Lizzie giggled.

"Pity posterity! They'll not believe in her. They'll think you made her up!"

"Who're you doing?"

"Mam. Dad. Gramma. Mrs Adams, I might."

"Nobody very interesting much, is there? Not *really* interesting."

The idea came to Lizzie then, ravishing in its power and simplicity.

"The witch!"

She must have said the word out loud.

"The—what?"

110

Lizzie was silent.

"Did you say *witch*?"

"I've a good mind to tell him," she thought.

"You did, didn't you?" he persisted. "You said it once before, as well. What d'ye mean, witch?"

Lizzie looked at him then, straight in the eyes.

"I mean—witch," she said.

It had been said at last. He sat up.

"Witch?" he said. "Witch? You're barmy."

"Oh, I know," agreed Lizzie, hiding her disappointment. "Nobody believes a single word I say. Didn't you know?"

She stood up.

"Where're you going?"

"You wouldn't believe me if I told you," she answered, and began to run.

"Hey! Lizzie!"

She took no notice. Clutching her wild flowers in one hand and the camera in the other she went pell-mell down the green lane between the high, scented hedgerows and white sprays.

"Lizzie Dripping, Lizzie Dripping,
Don't look now your fibs are slipping!"

She stopped and looked back. All was still. There was no sign of pursuit.

"Shouldn't've told him," she thought. "Wish I hadn't."

She walked on slowly. "Thing is, they won't believe it in 2090 either," she thought. "If they don't believe me now, with the witch just round the corner, they never will *then*...."

Another idea came, quite effortlessly. She lifted the polaroid camera and stared at it as if it were magic as any witch's spell.

"Ooh ... what if ...?" A photograph of a real witch, sitting on a real tombstone! Her witch, caught forever in the lens, inescapably a fact, for people in Little Hemlock now, let alone in 2090.

"I will!" she thought exultantly. "I'll do it! *Have* to believe in her then, they would—*and* that Jonathan, *and* the rest of them! Oooh—why didn't I think of it before?"

And Lizzie Dripping started to run again.

Five minutes later she was behind the east wall of the church.

"Better not let her see the camera," she thought. And then, "What's it matter? Won't know what it is, even if she *does* see it. Look funny, standing with hands behind me back. Just swing it—careless like. She won't know what it is. . . ."

She practised swinging the camera carelessly for a moment, then advanced.

"Do interview first," she thought, "then take photo at end. Might get mad, else."

A very small voice right at the back of Lizzie's head was telling her not to do either, either the interview or the photograph. But Lizzie was bent on securing that tricky witch *now*, for ever more, tying her down, pinning her like a butterfly. She pretended she did not hear the warning voice. She edged round the corner of the church, cautious even after so many meetings and so many conversations. The witch was there. She sat perfectly

112

still, her eyes closed, looking curiously blissful and at peace.

"Asleep?" Lizzie wondered. "Not sitting *up*!"

"Witch!" she called softly. "It's me—Lizzie!"

The witch gave a long, soft sigh and opened her eyes, reluctantly it seemed, looking dazed and far away.

"Doing a spell, were you?" Lizzie was awestruck by the very thought.

The witch nodded.

"I was—somewhere else," she said.

"Somewhere else? Just now? How?"

"Easy," said the witch. "Shut your eyes and be where you will. Easy, girl. Child's play."

"I s'pose it is," agreed Lizzie slowly. "For anyone really, not just witches. If you shut your eyes, *anything* can happen."

"That's right," said the witch. "You'll learn. You'll learn, my deary."

"Called me deary!" thought Lizzie. "Never done *that* before! Try her now, straight off, I'd better. . . ."

"Witch," she said aloud, "d'you think . . . can I ask you some questions? Just a few?"

"Questions?" All at once the witch was on guard again. "What kind of questions?"

"A sort of an interview," said Lizzie. "For a project we're doing at school. It'd not take long."

"Go on, then," said the witch surprisingly. One way or another she was being very surprising today. "Ask one. Not saying I'll answer, mind."

"Oh thank you!" cried Lizzie. "Thank you!"

She sat down then, with her back leaning against the comfortable tomb of Betsy Mabel Glossop, aged 79 years (*Life's Work Well Done*). She fished out her pencil and notebook and was ready, pencil poised. The camera lay by her right side in the grass.

"I know I've asked you this before," she began then, "but I really would like to know. What your *name* is."

"Not telling!" snapped the witch instantly. "What else?"

113

"Well, I—I don't s'pose you'd tell me—how old you are?"

The witch threw back her head then and cackled. She went on cackling and screaming for so long it seemed as though she would never stop. When at last she did, she fixed Lizzie with a glittering stare and chanted: "Time is now and time is then and time is soon and time is for ever and ever! For ever and ever!"

She flung out her arms with the last words as if she were actually holding time in her skinny palms, and scattering it like cold corn to the winds. Poor Lizzie sat nonplussed.

"And wherever time is," went on the witch, "there am I."

"So—so you'll still be here in a hundred years' time, then," asked Lizzie, trying to work it all out. "In 2090?"

"I already am," crooned the witch, smug and enigmatic. "I already am!"

"Oh," said Lizzie. "Oh."

She wrote in her notebook: *Is already in 2090.*

"Waste of time, asking her questions," she thought. But she had to try once more. Her next question was one she hardly knew how to ask, hardly *dared* to ask, even. It was one she desperately wanted the answer to, not only for posterity's sake, but for her own. She swallowed.

"Witch," she began, "witch, don't get mad, will you . . . ?"

The witch did not reply. She sat and hugged herself and rocked, and watched Lizzie.

"What I wanted to know is—well, what I wondered is—are you *real*? Oh, *I* believe in you, I do. What I mean is, if it's just *me* that sees you, you might not be *really* real, see. More like a kind of a dream or something."

She stopped. She knew that she had said it all badly. The witch sat and rocked on her wide stone slab and said not a word.

115

"*Are* you? Please witch—*please*?"

"She ain't going to say anything," Lizzie thought. "Oh, *why* won't she tell! Oh—I know!"

She suddenly remembered the camera and realised that she could force an answer of sorts, and quick as thought snatched up the camera, raised it, caught the witch in the lens and—click!

Lizzie lowered the camera.

"Gone! Oh quick—film!"

She pulled out the film and tucked it under her arm. Part of her mind was counting seconds, part racing with questions one after another.

"Gone! Why? For ever? Was it what I said? Was it—this?"

She drew out the film and peeled away the skin. She hardly dared to look. A gasp flew from her lips.

The photograph had come out well. It showed, black and white, the sun-flecked tomb of the Perfectly Peaceful Posts, the overhanging tree, the tall and whitening summer grass. What it did not show, not even as a smudge, not even as the merest blur, was a witch. For Lizzie, the shock had the force of a spell.

"Gone!"

The word, said out loud, was more bleak and true than it had ever seemed before. Lizzie looked down at the hateful photograph and back at the empty tomb and knew that she had betrayed her witch. By trying to make her real, she had made her unreal, had sent her into a silence and invisibility that might last for ever now.

"Oh witch!" Lizzie was close to tears. "I'm sorry, I'm sorry! Look!"

And she held up the photograph and tore it right across, then again and again.

There was no reply. Lizzie stared at the empty tombs and shivered because she thought she knew now that never would she look into those sour green eyes again, never hear that high cackle, see those stabbing white fingers. The witch had gone from Little Hemlock. The air, once thick with flying spells, was

116

empty now, ordinary air for breathing.

"I *am* Lizzie Dripping," she thought dully. "They're right. I am. . . ."

And Lizzie walked away.

". . . ever so many other things. Ever so many."

Lizzie lifted her head, came out of her dreaming. Aunt Blodwen was only a few yards in front of her, talking to Miss Platt over her garden hedge.

"Hello, Lizzie," called Miss Platt, and smiled.

"Hello, Miss Platt."

"Oh—Lizzie Dripping, is it! Where's Jonathan? With you, I thought, picking flowers."

"Oh, he was," Lizzie said. "Still is, for all I know."

"How are you getting on, Lizzie?" asked Miss Platt. "I'm col-

lecting so many things it looks as if there'll have to be half a dozen boxes, not just one."

"Oh yes, I was telling you, Miss Pratt," began Aunt Blodwen eagerly.

"Platt," corrected Lizzie and Miss Platt together.

"Platt—ever so many things. Me and Arthur on our wedding day—definitely let you have a photo of that, though I must say I like my hair better the style I've got it now. And then there's one of me taken at the seaside, judging a competition, would you believe, right next to the Mayor. Half a dozen photos of that I've got—in the newspapers it was, and my name on it and all."

"Why, thank you, Mrs Cole," said Miss Platt. "That would be nice."

"Well—thought it'd be something a bit different, see!" Aunt Blodwen gave a deprecating little laugh. "Can't imagine why they picked on me—all those thousands as there were—but there you are. Picked me right out from among them all and next thing I knew there I was right next to the Mayor and heaven knows! Wasn't I, Lizzie? Lizzie!"

Lizzie nodded grudgingly.

"Lovely," said Miss Platt.

"Mind, lovely idea of yours, Miss Pratt," said Aunt Blodwen. "Just to fancy—people in a hundred years' time to see that silly old photo of me with the Mayor! There *is* a photo somewhere of the flower arrangement in an egg cup I won first prize with at Mapleburn—1967 I think it was. Not one of my best, I thought. Bit limiting an egg cup, see, but there you are. I expect the judges knew best."

"Just hark at her," thought Lizzie. "Tin box to *herself* she'll want, afore she's done. Put her in a tin box, that's what I'd like, egg cups and all."

She started to walk off.

"Lizzie!" Miss Platt called after her, and she turned.

"Call round some time if you like, and see all the things I've collected. You could help me decide which to put in."

Lizzie nodded.

"Thanks. Yes, Miss Platt, I'd like that."

At the corner of Wellow Lane was a little group, who turned and watched her approach. Jonathan was among them.

"Lizzie Dripping, Lizzie Dripping!"

"Who believes in witches, then?"

"Look out, Lizzie Dripping—*witch*'ll get you— whooooeeeee!"

"Seen any witches lately? Look out—there's one behind you!"

"Oh, shut up, shut up!" cried Lizzie. "Let me alone!"

"Who believes in witches? Lizzie Dripping!"

"I don't, I don't!" she cried. "Let me alone. I don't, I tell you!"

She began to run, and hardly heard their voices following, and felt the tears run hot on her cheeks. At last she slowed down and brushed her arm across her eyes and thought "I do I do I do!" and beyond that thought was an echo of a thought: "You don't you don't you don't!"

During the days that followed Lizzie was always hearing that voice and always trying to prove it wrong. She went to the graveyard (despite Patty's warnings) three and sometimes four times a day. Even on wet days she went, and would crouch under the dry yew by the Posts' tomb till her knees ached and she felt queer and giddy from staring into the falling rain. She went out of a blind and dogged obstinacy, because Lizzie Dripping was not going to see that witch ever again. She knew it without needing to prove it, and yet was determined to prove it.

"I never said goodbye, even," she would think suddenly in the middle of doing a jigsaw or walking along on quite an ordinary errand. And straightaway she would go on searching again, sometimes to the graveyard, sometimes to the mill, the Larkins' pond—anywhere in Little Hemlock where once that witch had been. She even went to the ten-acre and tried her own spell again:

"Witch appear, witch appear,
I make you witch, out of the air!"

Time and again she said the words, time and again she plucked vainly at daisies—"witch, not, witch, not ..." And more than once she cried herself to sleep.

It was after a visit to the graveyard that she saw Miss Platt in her garden again, and was invited in to see the growing hoard of treasure for the tin box. On a table covered with a fringed red plush cloth they were arranged in tidy groups, every item numbered and entered in a stiff covered notebook.

"It almost makes you wish you could be there yourself when the box is opened," said Miss Platt. "Can't you imagine how excited they'll be? It makes me wish *we* had one to open. And the different things we've collected! Look at this."

"What is it?" Lizzie took the photograph.

"It's the first car in Little Hemlock. Mrs Draycott gave it, at the Post Office—it belonged to her father. And you know what *this* is, of course." She held out another picture.

"Us!" said Lizzie. "On that footpath walk! There's Gramma! Eeeh—and look at me—mouth stuffed full—will they really see *me* then, in 2090? Funniest feeling it gives you, don't it? We'll all be *dead*—even me—even Toby! It's not morbid to say that, is it, Miss Platt? It's true, anyhow. But Mam says it's morbid—*and* going into the graveyard."

She stared gloomily at the picture in her hand and thought again, inevitably, of the witch and that other ill-fated photograph.

"Is something the matter, Lizzie?" asked Miss Platt.

"Oooh," Lizzie hesitated. "I wish I could tell you."

"And can't you?"

"You'd laugh. They all do."

"I don't think I would. In fact, I'm sure I wouldn't."

"Even if you didn't laugh you'd think I was a fibber," said

Lizzie bitterly. "Everyone does. There's *nobody* I can tell, not in the whole world."

"It really is a secret, then?"

Lizzie nodded.

"I wonder—I wonder if it has anything to do with a witch?"

"A—how do you know?" Lizzie gasped.

Miss Platt laughed then.

"I'm not deaf, Lizzie. I think I already know that you go and meet a witch in the graveyard."

"And—and you believe me?"

"I think, Lizzie," said Miss Platt carefully, "that people's witches are their own affair. I don't for a single minute think that if *I* went to the graveyard I would meet your witch. Or that anyone else would, for that matter—except you."

Lizzie, to her dismay, felt tears springing.

"Only I don't see her any more!" she cried. At last she was able to tell. "Oh Miss Platt—she's gone, gone for ever. I know she has, and it's all my fault! And that old witch, she was smashing, she was ... oh!"

And now Lizzie began to sob in earnest.

"My friend, she was! And then I went and took a photo of her—wanted to prove she was there, see, really there, so's the others wouldn't laugh at me!"

"And she wasn't there," said Miss Platt. "At least, she didn't show on the photograph."

Lizzie looked up.

"Didn't show? You mean—she could've been real and *still* not showed on photo?"

Miss Platt nodded. "That's exactly what I mean, Lizzie. I believe she was real—to you."

"True, that is," said Lizzie. "Aye, that's true. But what I really wanted was to put her in't box, see, for 2090. So's *they'd* know about her."

"Ah—I see. Well, I think we can do something about that."

"But what? She don't *come* any more—I've been there dozens o' times—and to the mill, *and* to the pond."

"How do you know about witches, Lizzie?" asked Miss Platt surprisingly. "How did you know what one looked like, for instance, before you met your own."

"Know? Well—I—from books, I s'pose."

"That's right. That's how we all know. So you see there *is* a way you can tell them about your witch in 2090."

"*Is* there?"

"Listen. Tomorrow is the first day of term. And in the afternoon I'm going to ask you all to sing one or two songs—and one of them, as a matter of fact, is one *about* witches—the one we learned last term. And I'm going to record them, and then put the tape in the tin trunk. So what we'll do, is this. . . ."

Next day Lizzie left school half-an-hour early, the cassette recorder in her satchel.

"Lizzie is leaving early because she's doing something for me," Miss Platt had told the others. "Something special, for the 2090 box."

And the rest of them were still singing, Lizzie could hear their voices following, singing about witches:

"Oooooh! Oooh!
We crouch on Pendle Hill
When all the moors are still,
We feed on roots and moory moss and shale;
We weave our spells of spite
All through the creeping night
And skip and dance like scarecrows in a gale!"

Lizzie was making for the graveyard.

"Rather do it there," she had told Miss Platt. "It'll seem more—more real. And anyhow, if that old witch hears me, she might—well, you never know."

"You'll be making her real anyhow," Lizzie thought now. "Miss Platt says so. *And* she'll be real to them that hears the tape in a hundred years."

She went into the graveyard and climbed the familiar steep pathway into the sky and walked down by the side of the

123

church, not slowly or with caution as once she had, because she did not expect to meet the witch now.

She chose a place to sit under the yew, so that as she told her story she could see the tomb of the Perfectly Peaceful Posts. There she sat quietly for a moment or two drawing in the dry, woody smell, seeing the way the glinting ivy curled and remembering meetings, hearing voices.

"Where shall I begin?" she wondered, and placed the cassette recorder in the grass. "Right at the beginning, I s'pose, tell 'em who I am first. 'Once upon a time'—yes, that's how they always start. . . ."

Lizzie picked up the microphone, pressed the button marked "record", and began:

"Once upon a time—and I mean last week, or last year—there was a girl called Lizzie Dripping. . . ."

And so Lizzie began her story, and before long the witch was there again in her mind's eye, hunched and mocking and dusty and in some curious way more there, more Lizzie's, than ever before.

"... Lizzie saw the witch before the witch saw her. What the witch was doing, was sitting with her back propped against a tombstone—the one in memory of Hannah Post of this parish and Albert Cyril beloved husband of the above 1802 to 1879 Peace Perfect Peace. . . ."

It was a very long time before Lizzie had finished her story. She heard the church clock strike six and knew she had missed tea and did not even care. She stopped the tape, thought for a moment, and then started it again.

"And this is a true story," she said loudly and firmly. "Signed—Lizzie Dripping!"

Then she pressed the button that said *Stop*, got up, and began to walk away down the pathway from the sky.

also published by BBC Children's Books:

Lizzie Dripping and the Witch

HELEN CRESSWELL

The village where Lizzie Dripping lives, Little Hemlock, is quite an ordinary village with a school, a few shops, a church and a graveyard. Only Lizzie Dripping knows that it also has its very own witch.

Although Lizzie thinks of the witch as *her* witch, and a friend of sorts, she is a tricky customer. She comes and goes as she pleases, refuses to tell her name and is quite capable of turning cats into toads. And with someone like *that* living in the village, life is never dull . . .

also published by BBC Children's Books:

The Adventures of Arabel and Mortimer

JOAN AIKEN

illustrated by Quentin Blake

Arabel's Raven

Arabel and the Escaped Black Mamba

The Bread Bin

Mortimer's Tie

Mortimer and Arabel

Mortimer and the Sword Excalibur

The Spiral Stair

The Mystery of Mr Jones's Disappearing Taxi

Mortimer's Portrait on Glass

Mortimer's Cross